THE UNDEAD ATE MY HEAD

Ethan Nahté

The Undead Ate My Head
Ethan Nahté
First Edition Copyright © Ethan Nahté, 2017

Published by Yard Dog Press at Create Space

Print Version ISBN 978-1-945941-06-1
The Undead Ate My Head
First Edition Copyright © Ethan Nahté, 2017

Yard Dog Press
710 W. Redbud Lane
Alma, AR 72921-7247

http://www.yarddogpress.com

Edited by Selina Rosen
Copy Editor & Technical Editor Lynn Rosen
Cover art by Mitchell Bentley

First Print Edition June 1, 2017
First EEdition May, 2017
Printed in the United States of America
0 9 8 7 6 5 4 3 2 1

DEDICATED TO

My family
and to Lisa

TABLE OF CONTENTS

Attack of the Bumbies 7

Circle of Death 17

Flaming Yumbie 29

He Grumbled; She Bitched 37

Hillbilly Hell 45

Twinkie Trap 95

About the Author 117

About the Cover Artist 119

ATTACK OF THE BUMBIES

The sun was setting in a blood-red sky as Tracey was out walking Henry Dragonheart III, her Welsh corgi. The horizon appeared surreal, yet beautiful in its own sanguine manner. The salt air of the sea wafted its way to the quaint neighborhood in east Penarth. Tracey was returning to her little house at the end of the cul-de-sac when Henry began putting up a fuss, barking as if he had gone mad, pulling desperately at the leash.

Tracey turned, politely telling Henry, "Now, now Henry. You know we don't bother the neighbors with unnecessary noise and commotion."

She was shaking her finger at the dog as she chastised him, but the corgi paid her no heed. His stub of a tail was rigid and his hackles rose as he tugged at his leash. Tracey looked off in the direction her dog was barking and could see bipedal figures lumbering down the asphalt lane, as if they were lame. There were plenty of other homes they could've attacked, although Tracey wasn't aware that was their goal at the moment, but maybe they chose to follow her and Henry since they were the only living, breathing entities outdoors in that particular neighborhood at the moment. She rushed inside, nearly choking Henry as she pulled the barking dog behind her.

"Nigel! Nigel!"

"Blimey, woman, what's all the bloody racket about?" he asked.

"There are people, I suppose they're people," she said with a bit of uncertainty, "slowly making their way down the street, ambling as it were, following us. They're moving very strangely–hunting us it seemed."

"Well your days of being a hot fox are done and gone, so can't be fox hunters," he joked. He immediately tried to retract his comment when he saw the look in her eyes and thought his chances of survival might be better with whatever she was imagining coming down the lane.

"There'll be no pudding for you if we survive this," she said vehemently.

Nigel, feeling an urge to escape her gaze, looked out the window. The street lamps were just flickering to life but he could see the odd quintet approaching. They were still more than half a block away.

"Do you think they're shooting a new episode of *Doctor Who*?" Nigel asked his wife.

She thought for a moment, her index finger to her lip, before saying, "No, I don't think so. Last time they let the entire neighborhood know two weeks in advance before they had the Cybermen stomping down the street. Remember that posh bird coming around with release forms for us to sign?"

"Well I don't suppose it would be *Torchwood*, either, then. I would expect they would extend us the same courtesy," her husband stated. He turned from the window and went to the door, locking the keyed entry as well as the deadbolt. "Right, then. You go lock the back door and make sure all of the windows are latched tight. I'm going to get a few things to reinforce the house."

With that, Nigel rushed through the kitchen and out the door leading into the garage. He had a good variety of tools, woodworking being a hobby he fancied. He flipped on the power to the table saw to let it get up to speed while he began grabbing two planks at a time, dragging them nearer to the saw and leaning them up against the wall. He knew he didn't have much time. He figured each board simply cut in half should be sufficient enough to cover the span of the windows. No time to measure; a quick guestimate would have to suffice.

"Nigel," Tracey screamed a few minutes later, poking her head through the doorway to be heard over the saw. "They're at the curbside. One is dripping all over the mailbox."

Nigel killed the saw and gathered up the boards he had cut, pondering what his wife meant exactly when she said "dripping." He brought his payload through the door, dropping two or three boards here and there below each window and a couple of extra boards at the back door. He made his way to the living room where Tracey was peeking around the drapes and out the window. Henry was bouncing up and down on his front paws, barking incessantly.

"Henry, shush! Dear, what did you mean by 'dripping?'"

"Exactly what I bloody hell said, Nigel."

"Oi!"

"Well I couldn't make it any plainer if I were the nose on Prince Charles' face. The bloke, if that's what that, that thing is, sort of oozed and dripped body parts all over the box and across the lawn. My poor geraniums and sweet peas. What will Mrs. Hobbes think when she sees the poor condition that creature has left them in? I'll be ousted from the garden club."

"Blast your flowers, you daft ol' ninny. We've got bigger problems at the moment." Nigel, his curiosity getting the best of him, peered out the window. Two rotting corpses met his visage, mere inches from the pane, only the stand of holly bushes keeping the reanimated beings from pushing through for the moment.

"Here, hold this board," he said, hurriedly handing his wife the first of several boards to be quickly nailed up throughout the house. Occasionally they would hear glass breaking, forcing them to rush to the vandalized room to find a creature attempting to climb inside. Nigel walloped a couple as if his plank was a cricket bat, bashing in their heads, splattering bits of gray, red, and blackened globs across the carpet. Henry ripped the arm and entire shoulder free from one corpse before Tracey gripped the body, with potholders on her hands to protect them from getting ichor on them, and tossed the living dead abomination back through the window. She was quite *sturdy*, after all.

They finally made it to the last window, or what was left of it. Nigel drew back, taking quick aim as he slammed the hammer down on an already bloody and gnarled hand. The bones crunched and the flesh gave way, blood spurting from the wounds as it withdrew between the boards that Nigel and Tracey were putting up across that final window. Tracey took advantage of the retreating hand, placing one last board over the opening as Nigel expertly hammered in plenty of nails as well as a couple of extra just to make certain.

"It's a good thing the garage is connected to the house," Tracey said, exasperated as she wiped the sweat from her brow. Adrenaline and nerves had kept the young, married couple going during the attack on their home by the five strange looking people who seemed to be in a daze—and possibly deceased.

"Quite right you are, my turtle dove" Nigel replied, trying to get back on his wife's good side after making the fox remark. "Hammer and nails weren't a problem, but if it hadn't been for planks I had intended on using to build a new fence about the house then we would've been out of luck."

Human screams could be heard in the distance down the block. A delicate chime sounded from a clock on the mantel.

"Oh, time for tea and biscuits," Tracey commented.

"Perfect! Those vile creatures are locked out and I'm ripe for a breather. I'll turn on the telly to see if they've anything to say about the situation while we relax for a bit."

The familiar theme and logo of the local news played, interrupting a rerun of *Mr. Bean*.

"I'm Diana Faulkner."

"And I'm Ian Connelly, just outside of Birmingham at Castle Bromwich Hall with breaking news. We'll return to the attacks in Penarth once we have another live crew willing to go in and film the atrocities taking place."

The reporting duo had broad smiles upon their faces and a gleam in their eyes as they stood before the four-hundred-year-old castle. A crowd of onlookers stood on either side of them within a row of barricades. British Army personnel were keeping guard along the outside of the barricades, armed with automatic weapons as Klieg spotlights cut swaths across the lawn and gardens surrounding the historic castle.

The camera zoomed in on Diana as she continued, "Parts of Wales and the West Midlands, including Birmingham and the borough of Solihull, have been the scene of fantastic and unusual events as an angry red sun set this evening over the Atlantic."

"Of course, Diana," Ian said, smiling with a mouth that seemed to have more teeth than a human mouth could possibly contain, "the red sky is not an anomaly but more than likely caused by the amount of pollution in the atmosphere from all of the factories from nearby Birmingham, or Brum, as it is oft times called by the Brummies."

"Quite right, Ian," Diana said without looking away from the camera, still maintaining her smile. "It appears as though some, if not all, of the dead have exhumed themselves from their graves, leaving their cemetery plots and romping about the land of the living."

"I don't know if I would say romping," Ian interrupted with a chuckle. Diana returned his humour with her own chortle and snort.

The single cameraman, unused to two reporters on site, was having a hell of a time keeping up while shooting close-ups. He could've sworn that when Diana snorted the windscreen of her mic moved slightly as if at risk of being sucked up by her aquiline shnoz. The cameraman opted to zoom out and just go for the twofer.

"Yes," Diana said, cutting her laugh off as if it was switch-operated. Now her smile was a bit more forced. "I guess romping, though a colourful phrase, would be a bit inaccurate. The walking dead are not the fastest moving beings as they shamble and stagger through the parks, down the streets and into people's yards. But that hasn't stopped them from taking some residents by surprise and attacking them. Generally three or four zombies…"

"Or bumbies," Ian quickly blurted out before breaking out with a nerdish laugh.

Diana's smile faltered, just for an instant, before she regained her composure. "The zombies, or bumbies, are attacking residents as a group, killing most of their victims. The dead are being found in yards, homes, in the streets and even the workplace.

"It gives a whole new meaning to graveyard shift," said Ian.

Diana was no longer smiling, her lips a straight line and her expression stoic. "The military, which you can see on guard here behind us, is keeping an eye out all the way around the perimeter. They are especially keeping their focus to our northwest, in the direction of the Brooksfield Cemetery, which isn't too far from our current location. Not to mention the marshy area also to the northwest, near the M6, where archaeologists have found some bodily remains from battles past over the years. There's no telling what may still be buried out there—or was once buried.

"Unlike the zombies we are accustomed to seeing in popular horror films, these zombies don't seem to be interested in brains, necessarily. They tend to bite their victims on the bum first before making their way through the abdominal cavity and eating their way to the extremities."

"So, Diana, these Brummies are being eaten by bumbies." Ian began to laugh again before he let out a yowl and fell out of the camera's line of site as he hopped on one foot before succumbing to gravity and falling over. Diana's scowl returned to a smile, as she was obviously satisfied with the effect of her high heel upon Ian's shin.

The cameraman was just about to push in for a close up when Diana suddenly announced, "Oi, here's a surprise. Birmingham's very own Ozzy Osbourne and his wife and manager Sharon Osbourne."

The celebrity couple stepped into view of the camera, Sharon in an elegant, black dress and Ozzy, although not in a suit, dressed smartly with a large cross necklace dangling about his neck. Ian tried to limp back into the picture, but Sharon just elbowed him out of the way, never taking her eyes off the lens.

Ozzy turned to see the man crumple over and groan. He mumbled to Diana, "Who the bloody hell is that?"

"It's no one," she replied with a smile. "So what brings the two of you up from Buckinghamshire and back to Birmingham?"

"We were attending a dinner party with friends," Sharon answered. "We were about to get out of the car when a horde of people began pounding on the windows, then the roof and hood."

"We, we, we thought at first that it was bloody, fBLEEPing fans, trying to get a fBLEEPing autograph or some fBLEEPing shBLEEP, you know," Ozzy stammered, as the director quickly ordered the sound engineer to keep her hand over the "censor" button. Although the broadcast was on a three second time delay, prior experience with the infamous rocker was enough to make the director nervous. Ozzy continued, "But they were bloody fBLEEPing bleeding all over the fBLEEPing windows and shBLEEP, for fBLEEP's sake."

Sharon spoke up, commenting as tactfully as possible, "So our driver attempted to get us out of harm's way without running anyone down, but the mob was so thick that he finally just began plowing a path through the buggers. They didn't seem to mind, really."

"That sounds horrifying," Diana said. "Have either of you ever had anything of such a terrifying nature happen like this before?"

"What?" Sharon asked in disbelief. "Have fBLEEPing zombies attack and try to eat us? Are you fBLEEPing daft?"

Diana, who was on autopilot with her questions, blinked then realized the stupidity of her question. One could almost hear the cogs in her head turning as she tried to recover with something sensible. Fortunately, the rock star came to the rescue, whether he meant to or not, taking the pressure off of her for the moment.

"I had an acid trip once where mmrrmmrbble..."

"Oh, do be quiet, Ozzy," Sharon demanded.

"Of course you've never had the undead come after you before," Diana said. "I meant to ask have you ever had such a near-death experience with the fans attacking."

"No, never with the fans," Ozzy replied.

"So how is it that you arrived at Bromwich Hall?"

"In a fBLEEPing Rolls, of course," Ozzy said.

"Our driver," Sharon continued, trying to ignore her husband's remark, "went as far as he could go, but the bodies began piling up so deep and I believe the front of the car must've gotten buggered up to the point that it began overheating. We noticed the spotlights and military and made a run for it."

"Well thank God you're safe," Diana said, placing her hand on Ozzy's shoulder in a consoling manner.

"Well, we could use a, a, a, a doctor. Winston, our driver, seems to have gotten a bit of a scratch from one of the fBLEEPing wankers," Ozzy said.

"I'll be all right, sir," a weak voice said off-camera, his manners still shining through.

The cameraman panned his camera in an attempt to get a shot of the bleeding chauffer only to feel his elbow being held fast by the material from his shirt. He glanced around his viewfinder and saw Diana mouthing a few choice words to him, the gist being not to take the camera off her. God, he hated prima donnas. He panned back to the reporter, fake smile intact once more, and her celebrity guests.

"It was more than a bloody scratch," Sharon interjected. "The beast bloody well slashed poor Winston's neck. He's spurting blood all over that chap that tried to limp into the picture with us a moment ago."

"He, he, he resembles a bloody red wine fountain," Ozzy said.

"Nothing some alcohol and a couple of plasters won't take care of madam," said the weakening, if not proper, off-camera voice once again.

"Well that's good to hear," said Diana, who was feeling as if she wasn't getting as much airtime as she deserved. Granted, celebrities appearing next to her in the field would be great for her CV and reel, possibly getting her a desk job. But a chauffeur speaking somewhere off in the darkness was almost as bad as them pairing her up with a second reporter to work the story. She had to take back control of the interview before they cut away to another correspondent with something more important, like a physical bumbie attack. If there was to be any physical, live, on-camera attack, she wanted it to happen here so she could be the one to report on it. Tragic events were always ratings gold and did wonders for a reporter's popularity, even if she lost a fan or two due to their untimely demise.

"So tell me, what are your plans now that your dinner party has been ruined and you are possibly stuck here at the castle for the night? Some people are being allowed to enter the castle as a safety precaution, but it is filling up really fast."

"I can't fBLEEPing stick around here. I've got a new album I'm bloody recording starting next week."

"Which brings to mind," Diana said, totally shifting gears, "You recorded a song called 'Zombie Stomp' several years ago. Will this event bring any new zombie songs for the fans to enjoy?"

"The songs for the next album are all under wraps at the moment," said Sharon, her tone turning very protective of her husband-slash-client's work.

"Not meaning to tell you how to manage your husband's career, Sharon, but a zombie-themed album during these attacks would possibly be a big seller."

"If this zombie uprising is still occurring by the time the album is recorded, pressed and released, there won't be enough fans left to buy the bloody album, you twit. Piss off!" Sharon walked away in a huff.

"Well there you have it, folks," Diana said, unfazed and still smiling. "Even the rich and famous are not immune to the effects of the zombie—or bumbie—attacks."

A growling sound coming from very close by could be heard just behind the cameraman. Ozzy was yelling out, "Sharon," while he turned to see where his wife had stormed off to. He was still on the telly when the growl turned into a roar. Winston, the finely dressed chauffeur, came flying into the camera's field of view, launching himself at Ozzy from his blind side, and taking the rocker by surprise. Large patches of blood stained the left side of the chauffer's suit and shirt collar from the festering, gaping wound that had cut halfway through the muscles and tendons of his neck, just missing the vocal cords.

"Oh my God, does he normally look like that?" Diana asked as her smile turned to disgust seeing the visage of the man's graying skin and oozing sores.

The cameraman's calm, stationary style of shooting became more of a war zone documentary style as Ozzy and bumbie Winston struggled, the now-undead chauffeur grabbing Ozzy about the waist, trying to tackle the singer to the lawn. Sharon re-entered the scene once again, swinging her purse with all her force, slamming it upside Winston's skull, rocking the head and ripping even more of the muscle fiber loose. His grip upon Ozzy relaxed momentarily as he tried to regain his balance. Ozzy seized the moment, turning on his one-time dedicated chauffeur. He grappled the man from the side then placed his own mouth against the driver's lacerated neck.

"Ozzy, no" Sharon yelled, but it was too late. Ozzy had grabbed the dead man by the shoulder and head as he tore into him, biting with all his ferocity like the bumbie was a bat or some doves from back in the madman's checkered past. His teeth clamped down and ripped as his hands tore Winston's head from his body.

Blood smeared Ozzy's laughing and maniacal face. "Look, Sharon, I've still got it! I fBLEEPing bloody well showed him." He held the head up for the television audience to see as the body thumped to the ground. His laughter echoed across the castle grounds as onlookers gaped at the horror before them. A volley of cheers and devil-horned salutes went up into the air from approximately half the crowd.

Ozzy threw his arms up into the air, taking in the appreciation of the crowd as he yelled, "I can't fBLEEPing hear you! Louder!" The crowd roared even louder.

"Oh, put that disgusting thing down," Sharon said, a look of disgust upon her own face. "Ozzy, remember how much the rabies shots hurt? Just think about what they'll have to do to keep you from becoming a zombie."

"Bumbie," Diana interjected.

"Sod off, you twat," Sharon said as she flicked the V's.

"Look at it this way; if I'm undead I can fBLEEPing keep recording albums for decades. Ozzfest can go until the twenty-second century," Ozzy said with a smile, blood dribbling down his chin.

"You are such an arse at times. We'll talk about this when we get back home. What will the kids say?" Sharon dragged off Ozzy into the darkness as she chastised him for his spur of the moment shenanigans.

Diana snapped out of her temporary shock and looked back into the camera's eye, a splatter of the decapitated driver's blood dripping down her cheek. She lifted the microphone and said, "There you have it, the eternal Ozzy Osbourne, assuming all of the drugs he discussed taking in his autobiography *I Am Ozzy* doesn't make him immune to the zombie infection. Only time will tell if the Ozzman will have the longest record deal in the history of the music industry.

"Assuming we aren't overrun and eaten, we'll be back right after this commercial break."

The station cut to an advert. The cameraman relaxed his arm, putting the camera down by his side to give him a couple of minutes rest.

Ian was on the phone with the network producer, bitching at

him in a very high-pitched voice about not getting the equal amount of airtime promised and being upstaged, as well as bullied, by his cohort and unbooked guests.

Diana, on the other hand, was making a beeline for the production van, slipping in a pool of blood from the headless body of Winston. She caught herself, pulling Ian and the cameraman down into the remains while she managed to stay upright.

"Can somebody clean up this goddamn mess? And get makeup over here to get this fucking blood off of me before we go back live, for fuck's sake!" she screamed. Make-up and Hair came rushing over as Diana grumbled, "Bumbies, what wanker came up with that? This network has gone tits up."

THE CIRCLE OF DEATH

The Circle of Death is a tale similar to the familiar Circle of Life told by parents and teachers to the young, who will eventually tell it to their young and so forth. Though, in the case of The Circle of Death, it may not be told for many generations as those who live in that circle tend to be dead—and the dead tell no tales.

It all began when the European adventurers, explorers and pirates (which is really just another name for the explorers sanctioned and provisioned by a sponsoring country) came to the beautiful coasts east of the Amazon Jungle. At first the explorers were thought to be gods, but the natives soon learned they were demons. They became known as Anhangüera—old devils. As the Anhangüera made their way across the land, they raped and slaughtered more natives than they befriended. They tended to enslave any captives and forced their religion upon them in the name of God. Then the Europeans raped the land of its gold, timber and more.

The White Man spread his infectious diseases from tribe to tribe, killing men, women and children off even after they departed in their shining plates of armor with their spears, swords and magical tubes that flamed with black powder and exploded, unleashing a fury of death and devastation. The dark-skinned people felt as if they had angered several of their gods at once and were being repaid with a large, smiting hand from each deity.

Many died from fever, pox, sexually transmitted diseases, tuberculosis and such. Then there was the diminutive hunter known as Arpi who contracted the deadly living dead disease. Already ill with malaria, Arpi's encounter with the White Man proved disastrous.

Arpi had heard them approaching, as noisy as a herd of peccaries trampling through the underbrush to escape danger as they slapped at biting insects and cursed the forests. Like all of his tribe, Arpi knew how to disappear into the jungle, blending with his surroundings so fine that even animals would walk past him and not know he was there if he didn't want them to know.

Arpi's fever was what gave him away as he stood camouflaged against a Brazil nut tree. Despite trying to remain invisible, he broke out in a coughing fit, racking his lungs and ripping at his throat until he vomited up his breakfast, a mixture of bananas and brown spider monkey brains. Large beads of sweat crested upon his flushed face. Then he had a spear tip at his throat, forcing him to lift his head and look up into the eyes of three-dozen soldiers who appeared haggard. They too were sweating profusely in their armor and layer upon layers of materials.

One soldier who appeared to be the leader said something to Arpi, but Arpi couldn't understand what he was asking or that his lengthy name and title ended with Vasquez. The soldier kept speaking. Seeing that Arpi either couldn't understand him or was refusing to answer, the soldier motioned to his own mouth with his hand in a couple of different ways. Arpi finally understood they were seeking food and fresh water.

He nodded his head and pointed to the south, but that wasn't adequate. He was forced to show them, thrust into a tight group at the front of the cadre with a pike at his back. He marched the best he could, hacking and coughing, his spit and sweat spraying on some of the nearby soldiers. They would not let him rest, even when his coughing was so intense the ill Indian couldn't stand straight. Soldiers grabbed him on each side by his arms and forced him to keep moving. In doing so, Arpi's sweat combined with the blood of the soldier's cuts and scratches they had endured while traveling the jungle. Arpi's germs mingled with the Anhangüera's blood in a sickly brew within his small body, for Arpi barely reached five feet in height and didn't quite weigh a hundred pounds.

They reached a glade, a rare open space within the Amazon, not far from a clear-flowing stream and surrounded by many trees bearing a variety of fruit. Arpi pointed and told his captors they had arrived. They didn't understand a word he said but Captain Matéo Nicolas Pascual Vasquez voiced something to one of his men. The soldier stepped forward with hesitancy. He tasted the water and seemed pleased. The men cheered and Vasquez turned and patted Arpi on the back.

Arpi went into seizures, his body contorting and his head tossing to and fro. Blood streamed from his ears, nose and mouth before collapsing, falling down dead at Vasquez's metal-covered foot slicked with mud, muck and plant debris. Soldiers dragged the dead native a little ways off so his corpse wouldn't stink up their makeshift camp for the night or attract any wild carnivore into camp. The animals could eat Arpi at their own leisure without disturbing the soldiers and the soldiers would let the carnivores be.

But the carnivores did not eat the little brown man. They could smell something unnatural about Arpi and they all stayed clear of the body. Then the body rose from the forest floor deep in the middle of the night. The once living and breathing figure began to walk back to the glow of the small campfires of his former abductors.

Most of the soldiers were asleep, occasionally stirring as they slapped at biting insects. Only three were awake, standing guard. But the three were speaking with one another, huddled together on the edge of darkness but close enough to one of the small fires to gather some warmth, for there was a thick mist in the air that brought a damp chill that set painfully within their bones.

"This excursion is a death sentence," Cavazo hissed in a low whisper. "Vasquez is trying to impress his father and the courts where he holds office."

"Quiet, you," said Croucier. "His father is a very high-ranking official. He could have us hanged for your treasonous talk."

"What does it matter? We will die anyway in this forsaken jungle."

"We are all soldiers. Surely you don't think we will fall to a tribe of savages using sticks and stones? And even the captain is one of the best swordsmen in all of Spain, if not the New World, learning from the masters in Castile."

"Aye, but he is a coward. Notice how he stays clumped in the middle, letting others take point in case of an ambush. He fights before royalty and courtiers. His duels are with those that follow strict rules. He is not a man who likes to fight in the wild—the unknown raping his mind with a fear that almost paralyzes him."

"You should not talk in such a manner. I have no desire to forfeit my life because of your lies," Croucier said, turning his back on his friend, staring into the darkness.

They did not notice the soft, light footsteps of the undead Arpi approaching across the soft soil of the moist glade. The mist and gloom hid his walking corpse well enough. He had sliced the throats of two guards with daggers made from wood, stone and leather—primitive, but effective weapons he had made ages ago when he was a young boy and his father showed him the art of lethal craftsmanship.

The third soldier, Lorenzo Rodrigo Dominguez, began to cry out a warning as he drew his shortsword. His call was cut short as the small native launched himself at the guard's throat, his teeth tearing into the man's esophagus and unleashing a freshet of spurting gore. Before anyone could come to Dominguez's rescue, Arpi released the dying man's throat and raced off to the stream. He made it to the opposite bank and traveled throughout the night where the tributary he followed flowed into a larger river.

Arpi began walking through the deeper, larger waterway, but he did not make it far before red-bellied piranha attacked him. The sorely misjudged fish weren't predators as much as they were scavengers. Arpi was both dead and alive, so it was the best of both worlds for the piranha. Scores of the vicious bony fish snapped and snatched at his dead flesh. They soon devoured most of him, leaving little more than bones and cartilage with a piece of dangling meat attached here and there.

Back at the Spaniards' camp Vasquez was uncertain what to do. Every soldier who had been awake and could identify the attacker or explain the chain of events was dead, including two soldiers, the same two who had been forcing the native to march. They were lying next to one of the fires and had never stirred during the attack, having mysteriously passed sometime in the night.

Vasquez knew the attack was by a native, the evidence being the primitive knives lying in the grass near the dead guards. He had barely awakened and could just make out a small figure battling Dominguez when the dark figure disappeared, running off into the water and escaping into the jungle. He didn't know if more of the cannibals were about so he kept his men all in the glade, weapons at the ready.

The captain made it sound as if he didn't want his troop splitting up and weakening their forces. In truth, splitting his men up frightened Vasquez for it meant fewer soldiers to guard his cowardly hide.

Vasquez ordered the bodies stripped of anything useful and to bury them as fit for their journey to meet their Maker as they possibly could. He commanded a dozen of his men to do the tasks while the rest kept guard and made certain that nothing crept up on them for another assault. They made it through the night unmolested, digging shallow graves and covering the mounds with large chunks of dead trees to try and keep out predators, for there were very few rocks where they were. Small crosses were made and planted at the head of all five graves.

The next morning the soldiers refilled their waterskins. They ate fruits for breakfast then broke camp, in the search for more gold and glory, neither of which they had found much of on their sojourn. If they had stayed just a few hours more, they could've witnessed Dominguez rise from the dead alongside the two who had died in their sleep, Luis and Antonio—and they weren't hungry for fruit.

A very young black caiman quietly basked atop a dead walking palm tree. A thin layer of water covered the majority of the reptile's body, his eyes and snout the only portions visible above the waterline for the palm tree was partially submerged in a lazy segment of the river. Its massive root ball had been ripped from the soil, toppled during the last flood. The strong winds, rushing water and eroding earth finally won the battle the palm had fought for more than sixty years near the waterway.

The tiny predator resting along the dead tree was less than two feet long and was dwarfed by the palm's size. The caiman had gotten separated from its many siblings and now hunted and survived alone. At the moment, it lay motionless with the exception of its keen eyes tracking every minute movement. The reptile was starving. A plump bird, fat frog or juicy fish would be ideal.

He also had to keep a lookout for anything that might want to eat him. Caimans grew to be large and fierce predators and could take on anything in their ecosystem. As an adolescent, this particular caiman was just as much prey as predator.

A school of fish calmly swam towards the palm, seeking a shady area with a shoal. Some were reddish with gray and silver spotting their bodies and the younger fish more silver with darker spots. Either way, the sunlight hitting the water reflected brightly off their sleek forms. They had full bellies and were ready to rest somewhere out of danger's way.

They didn't find it.

Only one of their numbers was lost to the sharp teeth of the caiman. The attack was sudden. It was violent. It was over before most of the other piranha knew what they were fleeing from. It tasted—different.

The piranhas found a new shoal. The caiman crawled higher out of the water so he could take a nap, leaving the lower half of his body submerged in case he needed to flee, but high enough that the piranha would find it difficult to come back and attempt to eat him out of fishy revenge.

The sun reached its apex and the caiman slept fitfully, pain coursing through its scaly body. The afternoon advanced and the sun called it a night, allowing the moon to take its place. The orb's deathly pale light shone brightly on the river. Bats flitted about, swooping down near the watery surface to scoop up the denizen: insects, frogs and small fish. A cacophony of birds sang out and howler monkeys responded with their own calls, a contest of one monkey troop trying to overcome another troop across the water boundary.

The jungle was vibrant and alive.

Death was out for blood.

The caiman was awake and alert, the nighttime symphony a wondrous harmony that still enthralled the reptile. He waited patiently, observing an approaching tiger frog, wary of whether the brightly colored amphibian was poisonous or not. To eat or not to eat, that was the question.

The little frog crawled closer, paying more attention to the mosquitoes swarming about than the bump before it that looked like a part of the tree. The caiman was intent on its approaching dinner, throwing caution to the wind, deciding to eat it if it got close enough to snap between its jaws.

The frog hopped within range.

The caiman's body darted forward.

The chestnut red jaguarundi crouching in the nearby bushes sprang from its hiding place and caught the caiman in mid-leap as it deftly bounded over the fallen palm, landing in the shallows of the water with the thrashing reptile firmly between its teeth. The caiman twisted and chomped, attempting to break free. His sharp teeth caught the side of the cat's face with several ripping a gash that caused the jaguarundi to momentarily drop the caiman.

The tiger frog snatched a mosquito out of the air then hopped away and hid in the tall grass along the shore. It watched as a stealthy paw slapped down through the water, the claws piercing the underbelly of the struggling and injured caiman. The wildcat put her mouth around its dying prey once more then leapt out of the water and back to the safety of land. She chose to have her meal in a fork up a tree where she ate heartily, followed by cleaning her paws and the bleeding wound before resting. She generally hunted during the day, but today she had gotten a late start.

The infection set in as the feline slept and tried to recuperate. The wound became feverish and swollen. It was almost as annoying as the army of buzzing insects trying to get to her wound. They flew in and out of her ear. She became restless.

She struggled to push herself up from the fork. Once managed, she stretched, her tail flicking in the air as her front paws scratched and clawed at the limb before her. She heard the breaking dead twig just prior to feeling the tree shake. A much heavier body was bounding from the ground only to land and hurriedly claw its way just below her. She was clinging to the branch, now facing the tree as the spotted body came scampering up after her.

The jaguar had smelled the injured jaguarundi, her blood wafting in the air. The smell was bizarre and the jaguar didn't know what to make of it, but he knew he didn't like it. He tracked the scent across the wetland savannah, so much like a smaller version of the Pantanal way southwest of them. The jaguar found the origin of the unusual scent, a much smaller wildcat with red fur nestled in the crook of a bacuri tree. Something about the cat didn't seem right. Regardless, she was competition, a small predator in the jaguar's domain.

The jaguarundi knew she had to defend herself, but she was feeling dizzy and off balance. Her head was swimming and her fever blazing like being too close to the hairless ape's fire. She began backing away from the larger cat, one that outweighed her by two to three times as much. The jaguar had made it up to the fork in the branch where she had laid just moments before, the blood from her wound still fresh as the jaguar's front paw made its bloody mark as he pulled himself up to the branch.

The jaguar's teeth were fully bared as he lowered his head, sniffing and smelling her wound and her fear. He began testing the sturdiness of the branch, taking a hesitant step forward. The jaguarundi began moving back, further along the young limb that was beginning to bend under their weight.

The spotted predator advanced another step, its upper body weight fully supported by the stressed branch. The smaller cat shifted back more, alternating its guard of the deadly male in front of her and the ground a considerable distance below. The branch cracked. The jaguarundi scooted back a fraction more. The jaguar had three of its large paws on the branch and the fourth in the crook of the branch.

Monkeys, birds and a family of peccary hidden in the high grass were looking on from a safe distance, waiting to see what would happen. They could hear the branch crack again as the jaguarundi, her claws clenched tightly to the bark. It dropped a foot and bounced up and down with the smaller cat still clinging desperately.

The jaguar's mind was reeling, deciding what to do about the odd smelling cat it had cornered. There was nowhere for her to jump. He was hungry and she was an invader. He listened to his stomach and planted all four feet on the branch, his back foot smearing the jaguarundi's drying blood a little more.

The jaguarundi growled. Her fur was standing on end and her back was arching. She knew she was either going to have to bluff her way out or fight to the death if the branch held and she didn't crash headlong.

A howler monkey cried out way off in the distance, acting as the signal for action. The jaguar took another cautious step forward and the branch cracked even louder. The end where the red cat held on for her life dropped again. Now she was looking upwards at the jaguar as the branch was hanging at a severe angle. She noticed the jaguar preparing to move again.

The branch had enough and snapped, throwing the jaguar into the air. His mighty paws were swimming through emptiness as he was twisting his body, which was still close enough to reach the main part of the tree. He couldn't stop his fall, but he was able to penetrate the bark with his sharp claws, sliding— dropping—sliding some more—dropping again until he was a dozen feet from the surface. He let himself bound from the tree and spun his body, landing heavily in the grass, almost piercing himself upon the broken branch. He heard the squealing of the peccaries, the frightened monkeys and the alarm of the birds hastily flying away.

He stalked over to the other end of the branch. The jaguarundi lay beneath it, barely breathing with eyes half-closed. Her eyelids fluttered and the smaller cat exhaled deeply, its last breath brushing the hairs across the jaguar's snout. The jaguar sniffed the wound dealt her by the caiman and chose not to touch it. Instead, he sat up and began licking himself clean, all the way to his paws painted with dried blood.

As a reminder to other predators in his area who might smell the dead cat and check the situation out, the jaguar marked his territory, spraying the branch pinning the dead jaguarundi down. He stalked off into the setting sun. She arose before the dawn.

Captain Vasquez and his remaining soldiers were resting in small huts once occupied by a tribe that were now piled high a good ways downwind. The natives put up a good fight and had killed a third of his men with their blow darts laced with poison, probably from one of the small, brightly colored frogs the Spaniards had discovered in the Amazon. Stone headed spears or primitive bows and arrows had seriously injured a couple of his men.

But the explorers had overcome and killed more than five dozen men, women and children, plus a couple of mangy mutts. Vasquez hated that the wild pigs had run off during the battle. They would have made for a tasty supper.

Their reward was baskets and baskets of *cacahuatl*, the tasty cocoa beans that were worth a nice chunk of gold if they could get them back to Spain. He popped a bean down his throat, the contents giving him a little extra boost.

They also found several coca leaves, which if handled properly, made an unbelievable substance that made everything in the world seem right, gave those who partook of it a seemingly vast amount of immediate energy and could be applied to injuries to numb the affected area.

Vasquez ordered two men to keep guard of their cache. He ordered four more to keep watch on the village perimeter and for the guard to be changed every three hours. It gave everyone a chance to rest while still placing all his surviving men, those who could still stand, on watch while he would rest throughout the night.

It was the middle of the second watch, the morning sun still hours away. Although the moon was out and the clouds were sparse, the sky was nearly invisible to the soldiers due to the impenetrable upper canopy blocking out the heavens. The guards had a difficult time seeing into the dense foliage as well. They jumped every time a log popped in the campfire behind them. There were numerous howls, growls and things on the prowl that had them scared stiff.

One growl was sounding as if the creature was in pain more than on the hunt. The owner of the growl was on the hunt, smelling the pile of dead bodies on the other side of the camp it was approaching. The soft padding of his paws helped conceal his approach, but the pain that was striking throughout his muscular body was causing the jaguar to cry out unexpectedly. Normally he wouldn't be making a sound when preparing for an attack.

He saw the singular guard facing his direction. He smelled

other men spread out in separate directions from the one before him. He sprang from his hiding place, a move he had successfully made hundreds of times. This time the pain spreading throughout him struck as his back paws left the ground. His leap fell short. Instead of pouncing directly on his pray, the jaguar landed just shy, stumbling. His long body bowled the soldier over, knocking the man's weapon out of reach.

The sound of the man's armor crashing into the ground alerted the others on watch. The soldiers on either side rushed towards the fallen soldier. The fourth soldier guarding the side that faced the unceremoniously stacked dead bodies heaped upon one another kept his ground but had turned towards the camp to see if he could discern what was happening. The rest of the camp was coming alive with men waking and exiting their stolen huts partially clothed and unarmored.

He didn't see Dominguez, Antonio and Luis step from behind nearby trees. By the time the soldier realized he had company, it was too late. Dominguez bit a huge chunk out of the man's neck, one of the only places that wasn't covered by armor. The zombie ripped the man's carotid artery wide open. A fountain of blood sprayed along the trees and jungle floor as he screamed before succumbing to his future of undeath.

Antonio and Luis staggered their way around the fire, heading for the sleepy men exiting the huts to take on the undead jaguar.

Dominguez stalked towards the ensuing battle once he finished with the guard in front of him. A motion just inside the doorway of a hut to his left caught his eye. He paused and waited.

The jaguar was stabbed twice before its deadly claws ripped off half the face of the solider he had originally attacked. He also ripped out the throat of the soldier that managed to stab him with a pike.

The third soldier had slashed the jaguar across the ribcage with his shortsword, laying the cat open down the length of his spotted body. The crimson gore spread through the yellow, white and black fur. The jaguar retaliated, spinning quickly and tearing most of the meat and skin from the man's sword hand. The soldier dropped his sword, crying out in anguish as he grasped his battered hand. Two more soldiers with swords saved him. They backed the jaguar away with their yelling as they swiped and slashed at the beast.

Behind them, the other men began yelling and a new battle ensued as their former comrades in arms began savagely attacking, the blood and dirt clinging to their discolored bodies as they tried mauling each and every one of the unarmored men. Several living Spaniards went down, fatally wounded, before the two zombies were dispatched. The soldiers threw their heads and their bodies into the fire, fouling the air with the stench of flesh and rotting meat.

Ignoring the fight in the middle of the camp, frustrated and starving, the jaguar leapt for one of the newest soldiers swinging his sword. The cat's heavy body slammed into the unarmored man, all four sets of claws sinking deeply within his flesh. The jaguar's moves were a blur as he struck his victim several times, rending meat from the bone before the next sword blow struck him across his hindquarters. His victim had been partially rolled over and the jaguar struck quickly, snapping the man's neck, killing him instantly. The jaguar was satisfied for a moment. Then his own spinal cord was severed with the first blow of a sword. Two more blows and the cat's head dropped to the blood-soaked ground.

The survivors, having finished tossing Antonio and Luis on the fire, limped and straggled over to the commotion of the battle with the jungle lord. The only one who had not bothered coming over was the captain, a man who was prudent when it came to battle. He saw what was happening. Though he would grieve the loss of his men, primarily because it meant there were fewer soldiers to carry the treasure and some of it might have to be abandoned, he did value his own life and could see no sense in joining the battle.

If he had joined his soldiers, Dominguez might not have noticed Vasquez moving into the doorway of his hut. The captain was now the closest meal to Dominguez. The zombie had no cares about the ensuing fight on the other side of the campfire. His undead brain had simplified matters; first come, first served. He reached out from behind his former captain and grasped him around both arms, pinning them to his side.

Vasquez was startled and tried to call out to his men, but he couldn't be heard over the roaring fight he had been casually observing just moments ago. He was being drawn backwards into the jungle by an entity that never tired. His screams increased with his struggling, but he couldn't break free of the zombie's grip. He was taken all the way to the wall of natives his men had built. There, he felt the first bite. Dominguez clamped his teeth down between the captain's neck and shoulder, tearing the muscles in two. Vasquez was quickly learning the true meaning of pain.

The zombie bit him again, ripping Vasquez's ear off and devouring it whole. The frightened, spoiled officer whose father had bought him a commission was now swathed in his own blood. He was violently thrown to the ground, coming face-to-face with the dead chief of the villagers he had killed just hours before. The old man's open eyes stared at him with satisfaction, so it seemed to Vasquez.

He attempted to get up but his right arm failed him. He fell on his side, enabling him to see the face of his killer. The shock of seeing Dominguez's decrepit face hungrily coming for him paralyzed the captain. His mind wanted his body to run away, but his body refused to move. He twitched and mildly struggled as the weight of the dead body fell upon him and began gnawing at his gut, eating its way to Vasquez's innards. The captain's body was refusing to let him die, not until Dominguez made it to his heart. The painful bite ripped the aorta free. The blackness of the dark jungle faded even darker as Vasquez fell into oblivion and the New World disappeared.

The surviving soldiers knew their captain was missing but not one of the remaining men were willing to go out in the darkness and search for him. They discovered the disturbed ground where the captain's feet had kicked when he was first grabbed before being dragged off in the darkness. They called from the perimeter of the tiny village. After a few minutes with no reply, the men decided to wait until daylight to search for Captain Vasquez.

They found what was left of him strewn across the base of the dead natives. His eyes stared up in horror. Half of his head had been eaten away as had most of his torso. Flies and other vermin were feasting on his stinking remains. There was no sign of his killer. Just a couple of bloody footprints that petered out a few steps away, traveling off into the dense wilderness.

The downtrodden soldiers went back to their mosquito-infested camp to tend to their wounded and get some rest. At least that was the plan, but not everything always goes as planned when injured comrades and deceased companions become deadly enemies with a voracious and unquenchable thirst for fresh flesh.

And so the Circle of Death continues.

FLAMING YUMBIE

"Holy hell, Johnny! That one left an indent in the bottom of the mattress." Elton just snickered. Then he let fly with a retaliation fart that rumbled the bunk beds before wafting up toward the ceiling of the small bedroom located at the end of the single-wide.

"Sheeee-iitttt, Elton! I ain't gonna let my momma feed you no more pork n' beans when you come over to stay the night. Only if'n you're a comin' and a goin' back home to your own trailer, then I might let you eat beans over here." Johnny choked a couple of times between laughs, trying not to gag. He couldn't cover his face under the sheets because it smelled just as bad if not worse from his own farts as it did from the stench that Elton was cooking up on the bunk below a combination of pork, beans, barbecue chicken and venison jerky.

"So where was I?"

"You were just gettin' to the part about how the two girls heard a metallic clinking noise on the cabin window."

"Oh yeah, so then the two girls think that maybe the one-handed killer was watching them, so they decide to quit rubbing honey on each other's tits and put their halter tops back on."

"You are so full of horseshit."

"Is that any way to talk to your cousin?"

Johnny's reply was a reverberating rumble that was so potent it almost made the wallpaper peel and roll. "There's a little swamp gas to give your cockamamie story some flavor."

Elton and his asthma were so overcome by the most recent release of noxious fumes that he began gagging and choking. This resulted in the trailer shaking to and fro in a hurry as if a tornado was ricocheting off the sides of the mountains and the little piece of aluminum they were lying in was about to be spun off through the Ozarks.

But they both knew it wasn't a tornado. It was Johnny's dad and he was cursing up a storm all his own as he traipsed from the opposite end of the trailer and came tearing through the door. Both of the boys could see his oversized silhouette with the bright light from the hallway glaring behind him. His bulk filled most of the doorway, but there was enough room left between the doorframe and his thigh to notice the wide belt he held in his left hand.

"Johnny 'Little Bubba' Walton, do I need to tan yorn...*cough*...*cough*...and Elton's...*cough*... hides? Goddamn, I need to tell your momma not to fix no more beans for you boys."

Both boys tried their best not to smirk, smile or laugh as Johnny, Sr. choked back the tears that were welling up in his fumigated eyes. They knew this was the first (and last) warning of the evening, but if they cracked a smile right now, they might not be able to sit for a month of Sundays.

They felt the trailer shake a little more, like a rolling wave one might feel while sitting on an inner tube in the lake as a bass boat went flying by. Loretta Walton and all her bulk was preceded down the hallway by the smoke from her Pall Mall.

"Put that damn cigarette out, woman! These here boys have stockpiled enough gas in here to blow up the whole of Flustercluck County from them beans you made for supper."

"Johnny, you lissen' to yore pap and shut the hell up before he gets mad," she yelled from out of sight before turning and waddling her way back down the hall to the other end of the trailer where the master bedroom and her box of cupcakes were located.

"Sorry about that, pa. I guess the gas made us a little light-headed and gave us the giggles."

"Yep, sorry about that Uncle John. I couldn't get the window rolled out quick enough to get fresh air before my asthma kicked in."

"You wouldn't have asthma if that no good sister of mine hadn't married that insurance salesman with all his cheap ass polyester suits. I'd like to tie that sumbitch up to a telephone pole and flick lit cigarette butts at him to see how many it would take before he went up in flames." The last sentence was still audible even though Johnny, Sr. had slammed the bedroom door shut halfway through his tirade and was stalking his way back down the hall, making his way into the kitchen for a shot of Maker's Mark before kicking back and watching the wrestling match.

"Damn, that was a close one. My pa isn't anywhere near that scary."

"Cause your pa is a polyester wearing wuss like my pa just said. He ain't done nothin' but lie and cheat people."

"Oh yeah? What has your pa ever done?" Elton asked as he

saw his cousin leaning the upper part of his body over the side of the bunk and looking down at him like a possum hanging by its tail. He could just catch a glimmer of neon blue light reflecting off his face from the glow of the bug zapper hanging on the porch outside the room.

"Well I'll tell ya. You ever heard of a Flaming Yumbie?"

"No. What's that?"

"A Flaming Yumbie is the most potent drink throughout the Ozarks and possibly even the whole wide world," Johnny said with a gleam in his eye. "It all happened a few years back when you and I were just little kids. Pa was coming home from the chicken plant in his pickup truck one morning after working the late shift. He topped the hill over by ol' man Reid's shack when a doe and buck leapt right out in front of him. The doe got away but the buck hit the grill so hard that it smashed the radiator before flipping up over the hood, kicking in the windshield and landing right in the bed."

"Was he killed?"

"No he weren't killed. Who do ya think was just in here threatening to beat us, you idgit?"

"I meant the deer, you dumbass."

"Well sure enough he was killed. Pa just drove as far as he could before having to pull over and piss in the radiator. Then he drove a little further and made it to Big Coon Creek. He got a few empty beer cans out of the back of the truck and filled them with water and kept enough water in the truck to get her home."

"What's this got to do with a Flaming Yumbie?"

"I'm gettin' there. Just hold your horses," the boy said, a bit perturbed at being interrupted during his elocution. "So anyway, it was gonna take Earl more than a week to get another radiator in and to replace the windshield. And Pa heard on the CB scanner that there was a yumbie uprising going on over round Tater Hill. So he had to make a choice - take the three-wheeler, which had a double gun rack; or take the black '78 Trans Am, like the one in Smokey and the Bandit."

"Man, Sally Fields was smoking hot in that when she took off her wedding dress and..."

"Will you shut the hell up and let me tell my story?"

Elton picked his nose with his middle finger and flicked it at his cousin while giving him the bird all at the same time.

"So Pa tosses a couple of chickens out of the seat and tears ass out of the drive, throwing gravel every which way but loose," he said, smiling to himself for coming up with another cool movie's title that he could incorporate into his story. He hoped Elton had picked up on it but would keep his trap shut so he could finish his tale.

"He made it to the old fire road that goes up Tater Hill and noticed a couple of stray yumbies headed down a deer trail that crosses the road. He slammed on the brakes and spun the car around. Then he lifts himself up outta the T-top and unloads both barrels from his .20 gauge and just blows them bastards all to hell.

"Now the yumbies had been coming from the direction he was heading. So he got to thinking that maybe they was heading back to their hideout. So he drove up the fire road a few yards to get his car off of the main road and all, then he walked up to his kill. Sure enough, there was a deer trail there that had been used quite a bit most recently. From the dragging footprints and a stitch or two of business suit snagged by a briar or branch, Pa knew that he had come across a major yumbie path, a path so wide that he could drive down it. So he commenced stalking his prey.

"Amazingly enough, the path remained big and wide. Pa followed it deep into the woods even though darkness was beginning to fall. He came up behind a yumbie or two along the way and gave them each a load of buckshot, then he just drove over them and their three-piece suits for good measure.

"Finally, he saw a building off in a clearing a henhouse distance away from the road. The building was under attack by the yumbies. He called out a 10-10 code on the CB to let his buddies know a fight was in progress then gave them the 10-20. He fishtailed around and went barreling into the clearing, locking her up and sliding sideways, smacking four yumbies and sending them flying. They were part of a horde that had a group of men penned in like a warren full of rabbits. He reached behind the seat and brought out his secret weapon."

Elton's eyes were as big as saucers now. He was caught up in the story and clenching his fist, ready to get up and fight yumbies, himself. "What was the weapon? Did he have a Glock?"

"Hell no, you idgit. Pa had 'accidentally' brought back a flamethrower from back when he was in the third 'War on Terrorism.' He lit that puppy up and cut him a path all the way to the front door of the large building, which turned out to be an old hunting lodge that some ol' guy named Curtis Crow used to own.

After laying fire to a bunch of yumbies, the remaining critters high-tailed it into the woodwork for a few moments.

"Turns out that the lodge had been taken over by a bunch of locals from the next county over. They found the place abandoned and had started up a private club serving homemade shine, stolen beer and even had a pool table set up. Seems that Curtis used to bring rich hunters up here for deer, bear and razorback hunting, so this lodge was bigger'n most.

"Now pa was a bit miffed about this for a couple of reasons: One, none of Flustercluck County was told about the place; Two, he hadn't thought of it first. So after the group of penned-in Bubbas got to thankin' him for saving their mangy hides, he tears into the leader wanting to know why in the hell Flustercluck wasn't told about this here establishment.

"About this same time, two four-wheel drives had shown up loaded with men loaded with liquor, shotguns, rifles and a pistol or two. They was a might bit put out about the whole secret club thing, as well. They agreed to help the 'club owners' only if they could become members and use the lodge as well. The outsiders weren't looking to do no sharing. A fight broke out between a couple of the guys which ended up starting in the bar, proceeded through a window and ended up out in the clearing. But the fight was hard for anyone to see because it had gotten really dark by now and a thick mess of clouds hid the moon. A few guys had grabbed their lanterns and flashlights in one hand and their shine or beer in the other, but it wasn't enough light to see the yumbie waiting behind a nearby oak. The man from Flustercluck knocked his opponent back into the woods. Before anyone knew what had happened, a yumbie reached out and plumb ripped the man's head clean off."

Elton's jaw was almost on the floor. He was so entranced that he had backed himself against the wall against the bunk post. "Them other guys were stubborn ol' asses. Served them right."

"They came to their senses right soon enough. They hastily agreed to equal usage and then the fight betwixt men and yumbies began all over as the yumbies smelled fresh meat. Not everyone had his gun in his hands any longer since they had been inside drinking and discussing the rights of the land when the fight managed to break loose to the outside. So even though the number of yumbies versus the number of people was about the same, the men were outnumbered because most of them didn't want to get close enough to a yumbie to even risk getting a scratch and possibly become infected, and they didn't have time enough to run back in the lodge.

"Pa shouted out to the group to head to the ridge about a klick east of where they were. He told Harley and Jeb to take a keg of powder he saw in the lodge and a couple of bottles of shine, ordering them to leave a bottle at each end of the thin cliff trail on the ridge and to pour as much of the gunpowder as they could between the two. So off'n they went along with the rest of the men while Pa let fly with a couple of deadly blasts from his shotgun to cover their exodus. He then laid another path of fire across the front row of the encroaching maggots, which bought him enough time to reload the shotgun and to give his buddies another minute or so lead-time.

"Now yumbies, being as dumb as they are, had almost forgotten the other men and were keeping a watchful eye, which for some that was the only eye they had, on Pa as he bounded from one tree to the next, getting the yumbies to quit focusing on the trail to the east and to look a little more northeast just to buy some more time. But he kept himself within easy reach of the trail for when he figured it was time to high tail it outta there. He knew he had to give them enough time to lay the trap as well as the fact that he had to run a little slower to keep from catching up to them and to let the yumbies have a fresh trail to follow. Otherwise he would just flat outrun them and they'd never show up for his big surprise."

"I know what he's a planning," Elton said, so excited and sort of bouncing right where he sat that another fart slipped from between his cheeks, startling him.

"Well you may know, but what he planned and what happened ain't exactly the same thing. So zip your orifice. Both of 'em.

"So after a few more minutes, Pa decides to fire his last two shells into the two yumbies that were so close that he could smell the patent leather shoes they was wearing. One more yumbie was pretty close and he swung the gun by both barrels so hard that it broke the stock as it smashed that yumbie's head right in and plastered ooze all over the yumbie beside it.

"Now all he's got is the flamethrower and the skinnin' knife he always carries. He begins running down the trail, trying to see where he's going and taunting the yumbies, telling them their mothers were maids and their fathers were sharecroppers, just to keep them good and pissed off so they'd stay interested and follow. Once he gets to the sheer cliff wall and the thin trail that follows along it, he sees Harley pouring the last of the gun powder and Jeb setting the bottle of shine right at the edge of it. Pa scooted the other bottle over against the wall and behind a small rock to keep it from getting kicked off by the yumbies when they crossed. He then raked a little of the powder over to meet up more with the bottle. Then he called out one more time to the yumbies, telling them that they were all born from test tubes and that his squirrel dog had a better pedigree than they had.

"So once he made his way across the treacherous trail, the leader of the yumbies was just making it to the beginning. A bunch of the men were yelling obscenities, flipping the bird and dropping their pants to show their asses and get the yumbies to come across. There were only a couple of dozen left and it took a long time for them to all get on the skinny trail and past the first bottle. A couple had a misstep and took a tumble which was all right in Pa's book."

"Your pa wrote a book?"

"No, you boogerhead! He don't even own a book. As I was saying, fortunately the trail was rather lengthy and could hold that many people and still not have yumbies meeting up with my Pa face to face.

"Once Pa saw they were finally all on the trail he knelt down and took aim with the flamethrower. He pulled back on the trigger… but only a small flicker came out the end."

"Like this," Elton said as he stuck a lighter to his ass and lit a fart. Flames shot six inches from a hole in his underwear, damn near catching the sheets on fire.

"Nope, not even that much of a flame. He tried it again, but nothing came out of the muzzle. He was F-U-C-T, fuct! So he turnt on one knee, yelling for a shotgun as he tossed the flamethrower to the feller closest to him. A Winchester .410 shotgun crossed through the air. It wasn't much, but it would do, or so he hoped. He took aim but wasn't able to get a good bead on the bottle. The powder line was all a mess but the powder was still close enough, as thickly as it had been poured, to be somewhat consistent. So he did the next best thing and aimed for a spot a few feet above the bottle, a small rock ledge about seven feet up and a couple of feet in front of the shine.

"BLAM!" Johnny yelled out so suddenly that his cousin reared back, knocking his head into the bunk post. He was glad he didn't have a dip in his mouth or he would've swallowed it whole. He was also glad that Uncle John wasn't hauling ass down the hall to beat them senseless. Odds were that he had fallen asleep while watching wrestling and would've thought that the loud sounds were from a match.

"The shot ricocheted off'n the ledge, smashed the bottle of shine and an explosion of red and orange and yeller flames went roaring up and cut a jagged path down that cliff trail. A wall of flaming yumbies was a howlin' and hollerin' as they burned, knocking into one another and falling off the ridge, bouncin' off'n every rock and boulder and into the canyon below. He said it was cooler than watchin' a large beetle getting smoked between the wires in the bug zapper."

"Coooolll," was all Elton could say, a look of wonder upon his pimpled face.

"So once they got back to the lodge they mixed a pitcher of moonshine with a pinch of black powder, lit a match across the top of it and served it up as a Flaming Yumbie. Course, ya gotta put the sumbitch out before ya drink it so it don't blow your face off, but it's said to have a helluva kick."

HE GRUMBLED; SHE BITCHED

"All I know is that she-devil went all psycho hose beast on me last Monday while I was mowing the grass." David Joe shook his noggin vigorous like and took a swig of beer.

"Well, Bud," which is what everyone in Clovis County called David Joe due to his "horticultural" talents. "Maybe she was having the painters in," suggested Junior, Jr. His pa had been named Junior and folks thought he looked so much like his pa; fat, bald and drooling, when he was born they decided on making him Junior II, but that seemed awful fancy. So Junior, Jr. he was called.

Bud cracked another top off a beer bottle with the few teeth he had left on the right side of his mouth. "First of all, I's the only handyman there and secondly, what the hell do painters have to do with the story I's a tellin'?"

Junior, Jr. rolled his eyes and sighed, "I *meant* maybe she was riding the cotton pony."

"Dammit, Junior, Jr.! Ain't you lissened to a gawldarned word I been sayin'? The crazy bitch ran up on me from behind. Normally she wouldn't been able to up wearing them fancy heels she's always a clacking around in, but the roar of my John Deere Cutter 320 with the eight position blade cutter, the turn-on-a-dime..."

"I know which damn riding mower you got! We brought it home from the store in my pickup, you assjack."

"Well anyways, she grabs the hankie tied around my neck and yanked me plumb off the seat and over the back of the mower. Wasted a freshly opened brew."

"I understood all that. What I should have plainly said is maybe she was P-M-S-ing."

"Oh, Courtney, thank Lord & Taylor's," Tiffany cried.

"Did you hear? They shut down as well. Seems they found everyone at the Megamall either dead or being eaten by the Gamestop and Apple employees."

"I hope they ate that slut Bree Kostotos. She refused to let me return that turquoise ball gown just because I wore it twice," Tiffany snarled.

"How did she know?"

"She saw it on the bedroom floor when she walked in on me and her husband. Not like I got it stained or anything like that."

"What about the second time?"

"I had to wear something back home when I left."

"Oh, yeah," Courtney said, turning her head in a similar fashion to that of a dog when it's got a questioning look.

"So anyway, after attacking what's-his-name..."

"Bud."

"Whatever. I couldn't figure out what came over me." Tiffany took a moment for dramatic purposes as she daintily quaffed her sweetened, lo-fat cream with mint chip frappucino. "I tried calling Savannah, Cheyenne, Swoozie and you..."

"But me first, right?"

Tiffany pretended that she burnt the roof of her palate. "Why, yes, of course. Always my B-F-F first." Courtney smiled, too dumb to pick up on the diversionary tactic. "But my damn Black Touch Berry Pod wouldn't work. It's like the entire civilized world came to a halt."

"Tell me about it. No TV, no shopping and the electricity keeps flickering. It may not last us much longer."

"Not to mention all the rotting bodies everywhere."

"Is it just me or have you been craving more than flavored coffees and pâté?"

"Come to think of it, I actually licked the brown rivulets of sweat off of that dumb hillbilly's forehead once I had him on the ground. Normally I make him jump in the pool first and then I turn out the lights and close the blinds before allowing him to even get near me."

"I can't believe you let that redneck touch you."

"Hey! Don't be judging! I don't mind being a tramp if it'll save me some money. Besides, he cleans the pool for free afterwards. And what Chaz doesn't know isn't going to hurt him."

"Aren't you afraid Chaz might find out and..."

"Attack! Look out, Junior, Jr. It's Tiffany's live-in boyfriend."

"Thought you said he was a pussified, glass-jawed wimp?" Junior, Jr. was wrangling Chaz around the chest from behind, pulling him off Bud who had fallen through the lawn chair he had been sitting on.

"He is in what I believe to be a fair fight of eye-gouging, groin-kicking and a reverse suplex or pile driver. I weren't figgerin' on the maniac trying to eat my damn brains."

"You're right, there. That's the last thing any of us would expect."

Bud took the broken aluminum frame of the lawn chair and bent it some more, producing a makeshift spear. "Duck," he yelled.

Junior, Jr. held onto Chaz but ducked his head low. Bud reared back then slammed the pointed tip through Chaz's open maw, ramming through his throat and – it stopped – then bent. The cheap aluminum punctured the tissue and brain but broke down when it collided with the skull. Chaz fell forward, landing face-first on the aluminum piece and buckling more of it into his mouth. It matched his adult braces. His left hand clawed at...

"My ankle!" Tiffany screamed as she swatted little Ian McPhereson away with a fierce backhand. The diamond in her ring sliced his cheek open to the bone.

"Tiffany, you can't swat a child. Not in public, at least."

"Oh, hell. All these dead people around, whose going to notice one more little spoiled shit missing?"

"Actually, that's the only child I've seen since this happened. That little snot won the state spelling bee and skipped a grade."

"You notice that bratty little Kendall, whose mom is always bragging about her, didn't survive. Bet this all has to do with..." She whacked the shit out of Ian as he stumbled back over to her with his arms outstretched. "Intelligence. Maybe only we people with higher I.Q.s survived."

"That does explain what happened to all of my upper management dying off where I work."

"Although that doesn't explain why..." Tiffany was trying to come up with his name.

"Bud."

"Yeah, why he's still alive."

"Maybe he's like that old movie with Tom Cruise and Dustin Hoffman."

"That sorry sack of..."

"Shit! Another wasted beer due to some high fatootin' yuppie."

"It's worse than that. Check it, Bud. His arms and side of his neck look like road kill that's been sitting out a day or so. If'n I didn't know no better I'd say this guy had already been dead and was trying to eat us."

"Like a zombie?"

"I do believe so. Hell, he's got more horseflies and gnats following him around than Ned when he ain't bathed in a couple of seasons."

"Smells even a bit more rank now that you mention it."

"We gotta warn everyone. You call a kegger, show everybody the evidence and gather our ammo."

"What are you gonna do, Junior, Jr.?"

"I'm gonna hop in the four by four and do some of that there recon like sarge used to call it. I figure if'n I'm high enough in that truck and it's got a cattle guard on the front I can damn near see and run over anything which threatens me or gets in my way."

"Check on Tiffany, first. It's Thursday. She's probably down at that fancy coffee shop whining about something. But save her for me."

Tiffany made a hopeful attempt at using her phone. No signal, which didn't make sense to her. People or no people, the cell towers should still work – unless the phone company got overran by Bubbas and shut down.

"Who are you trying to call, Tif?"

"Chaz. I want to get his take on this. He works at a chemical lab. Surely he knows something about what's going on."

"Maybe they can create a better perfume or deodorant. I went swimming in my pool to try and cover this stench and it just won't go away. I smell like brie going bad."

Ian got back up once more, this time chasing after a tabby racing down the sidewalk in front of the coffee shop's patio. The cat turned and hissed before leaping in front of an on-coming Lexus. The driver swerved on reflex, overcompensating. The grill smashed right into Ian's skull, smacking it like the plunger on a pinball machine. The body smashed into a tree, the ruined head flew through the air and bounced across Tiffany and Courtney's table, crashing into their drinks and splattering them with coffee, whipped cream, eyeballs and icky bits.

Tiffany launched herself from her chair screaming bloody murder. She raced over to the Lexus, threw open the door and grabbed the woman who was applying lipstick in her vanity mirror. The woman was shocked by the rudeness of Tiffany's intrusion. It was obvious by the look in her eyes even after Tiffany had ripped the rotting head from the blackened neck, which seemed to be barely holding the two together to begin with.

"Tiffany! What are you doing?"

"The bitch's head was barely on, anyway. If this is to be our world then it's kill or be killed. I want brains and this bitch was short on resources and just going to be competition for us later on."

"Okay, whatever you say. Although she did ruin my brand new Versace by hitting that little zombie child."

"Zombie? Is that what we've become?"

"Yeah, totally. It's like M.J.'s 'Thriller'."

"Well at least we'll be able to dance. Let's go hunt us down a trailer park. Where do those sorts of people live around here?"

"We never drive to the west side of town. Maybe they're over there."

"Makes perfect sense to me."

Bud was spraying Bactine on his neck where he had a few claw marks from Chaz's ambush. He heard the roar of Junior, Jr.'s Chevy and saw him from eye level out the window of his trailer. Junior, Jr. had a pretty dandy lift kit on his truck and some monstrous tires. He heard the horn playing "Dixieland" just as he was slapping some gauze over the wounds. He walked to the living room and opened the screen door.

"Hey, Bud, tell 'em to meet in a couple of hours to give me time to..."

"What the hell?" Bud pointed to a black Mercedes barreling down the circular drive of the trailer park. Tiffany was behind the wheel and Courtney was hanging on to the "Oh, Shit" bar, trying not to end up in Tiffany's lap.

"Who the hell is this crazy bitch?"

"That's her, Junior, Jr. That's Tiffany. She's come to eat us."

"There's his truck," Tiffany said. She gunned the engine, aiming for a spot behind Bud's truck, sliding in the pea gravel and damn near going under the bumper of Junior, Jr.'s truck. The car kept sliding sideways, throwing gravel like shrapnel as she slammed into the family of ceramic deer that decorated the front yard. Shards of antlers and hooves sprayed and pinged off the trailer house and Bud so hard that he dropped his freshly opened brew.

"Look what the hell you did to my ten-pointer *and* my beer! Woman, what in tarnation are you doing here," Bud asked as Tiffany practically flew out of the car.

"I don't know what's going on but I'm sure you and your ilk

have something to do with it." She grappled his shoulders as he tried to hold the female wildcat back. "I'll be damned if you inbred pieces of trash are going to survive and repopulate the world."

"Like hell," Junior, Jr. replied as he reached behind his head to take the twelve gauge and the nine-millimeter rifle off the gun rack. Before he could get out of the truck Courtney was at his driver's side door. Tiffany was flailing away on Bud, her passion red nails clawing for his throat.

"You care what happens to these walking bags of rotting meat?"

Bud gasped and managed to wrench the extremely strong grip from around his windpipe. "Fuck, no!"

Junior, Jr. smiled as he released the lock on his truck door and kicked it open with such force it caught Courtney by surprise. The handle belted her across the bridge of her silicone nose, tearing it from the decaying flesh hidden beneath L'Oreal's base ninety-two to hide blemishes. Her nose hit the ground and small spurts of blood pumped across her make-up splotched face. She resembled what Michael Jackson might've looked like after a scuffle with Bubbles for inappropriate banana behavior.

Courtney's scream caught Tiffany's attention. The moment she turned her head was all Bud needed to break free, hit the ground and roll, just missing a dog turd. He quickly gained his feet, meeting Tiffany in her repeat attack. He lifted the ceramic antlers he had managed to grab during his roll. Four of the ten points were still intact. Tiffany couldn't check her momentum in time, ramming herself head on to the decorative projectiles. Her stomach and bits of intestines burst with the methane that had built up in her dying body.

"You white-trash piece-of-shit! That's going to ruin my ability to wear a two-piece at the beach!"

Bud shoved and twisted the horns a little more, ignoring the physical beating he was taking as she clawed and pummeled away at his head and chest. Her strength finally ebbed and she collapsed to the ground.

"Tiffany? Tiff?" Courtney, so caught up in her B-F-F-s possible demise, was oblivious to the cocking of both barrels of the .12 gauge just inches from her new perm. The blast sent fragments of skull and a bit of brain matter all over the side of the trailer owned by Melvin Hubbard.

"Shit, ol' Melvin ain't gonna be happy about me repainting the backside of his trailer."

Bud walked over, popping the top on two fresh beers. "Better than those damn zombies redecorating the inside with his innards."

"Point well made. Cheers," Junior, Jr. said as the two buddies clinked bottles and downed the cold brews all in one swig, each topping it off with a roaring belch.

They tied the corpses to the hood and took off through the trailer parks and Walmart parking lot to let the world know that changes were coming.

HILLBILLY HELL

The runoff from the hog farm ran rampant through the karst cave system, all thanks to an *overlooked* leak during a routine inspection. The inspector discreetly shoved a wad of green into his pocket upon his departure, which he hadn't possessed when walked onto the CAFO with a half hour earlier. The farm brought in a large sum in taxes for the rural area where the steep mountains and forests prevented industry and businesses from entering unless it was a small mom and pop shop or cafe in the center of the nearby communities that were almost too miniscule to even be called a town. That's the way the locals liked it—no outsiders unless they were only visiting for a couple of hours as they traveled on through.

Most of the locals had roots going back more than seven generations and their xenophobia was as much a part of their DNA as their mutated genes caused from a little loving from a close family member here and there. Some of the family trees looked more like a utility pole than a hundred-year-old oak. And they preferred the lack of visitors because it cut down on the potential of being caught poaching or growing things in their garden that the government looked down upon.

The hog farm had quietly slipped through the state's department of environmental quality, only coming to the public's attention after the permit was signed and the hog farmer had set up his operation. It was located extremely close to a national river system and in a rocky and mountainous area that was like a bee's honeycomb just a few feet beneath the soil where underground waterways and the rain runoff coursed through, coming out directly in the river or in small, nearby tributaries. The environmentalists couldn't do much about it except argue because the permit had already been allowed. The director of the department retired for undisclosed reasons, but the damage had been done.

The waste from more than 5,000 hogs collected in various tanks and, at times, those tanks would obtain a small tear. It's hard to see a leak in a tank that's filled with hog shit, and no one really wants to get into the offal because the smell of hog shit doesn't come off anything it touches regardless of how much its washed, sanitized and scrubbed. Burning a shoe or clothing that's been in hog shit is about the only way to get rid of the smell.

On the other side of the tributary below the hog farm was a local farmer who grew corn on a commercial level and baled hay for his own livestock as well as to sell. This year he tried a new pesticide to protect his crop of genetically enhanced produce. The karst cave system ran beneath his property just the same as the upwind hog farm that was currently producing an awful stench. The farmer was gagging as he tended the cornfield and saw his cows off in the distance moseying over the tallest hill on the property to get away from the smell. When a herd of animals known for producing a shitload of methane on a daily basis moves away from a foul stench, it might be time to pack one's shit and go.

It was an extremely hot and humid day, as it had been for the past two weeks. Temperatures hovered in the low 100s and the heat index rose above the mercury to 115. There had been no significant rain for three weeks and the tributary between the farms was low, pooling here and there around the bends and along the rocky shoreline. It was the perfect breeding ground, allowing mosquitoes and other bugs to lay their larvae in the mini-cesspools.

On a moonless August night an armadillo, whom was called Ernie by his three brothers and sisters, drank from one such pool, unaffected by the rank smell of the tepid water. Ernie drank heartily, nearly draining that particular puddle before wandering off in search of more food.

Two hours later, the banded creature emerged from a heavily wooded area, crossing through a ditch filled with dead grass, leaves and the rotting remains of a coon covered in maggots and other insects squirming in and out of desiccated flesh as they slurped up fluids busting from swollen pustules. The armadillo sniffed at the remains but decided to move on. The armored creature might be one of the only animals capable of transmitting the disease that causes leprosy, but that didn't mean it really wanted a meal of something as far gone as the coon's corpse.

Ernie waddled up the ditch and stepped onto the warm asphalt, unaware of the sports car flying around the curve twenty miles over the speed limit. His sense of smell and hearing was great but like the rest of his kin, Ernie's eyesight royally sucked. By the time the headlights illuminated the armored shell, pig-like head and armored tail sparsely covered with hair, it was really too late.

The driver, Sonny Teague, was slightly inebriated and the pitch dark road—a blacktop with no moonlight shining down and surrounded by trees to block any other light, if there had been any—made for an eerie but peaceful drive. Sonny hadn't seen another vehicle for probably an hour. It was late and a weekday. Most of the people around here who did work, which were few, either had farms or were loggers, so they went to bed with the chickens and woke up before the sun topped the peaks.

Sonny wasn't sure what the hell was in front of him, but he attempted to swerve about the time he was directly over Ernie. Scared shitless, Ernie jumped upwards, which armadillos tend to do when frightened. There's probably a scientific reason for their behavior but it all boils down to the fact that they are just dumb as fuck.

The boney armor slammed into the fiberglass bumper and was immediately slammed back down before the passenger side front tire. Sonny heard the bumper thumps then felt his car roll up and over the body. The mid-life crisis convertible crushed the shell just enough to puncture Ernie's internal organs and make for a really bad night. The back tire finished the job and Ernie thought, *Damn, should've had me a little coon for my last meal.* Then he gurgled and a bloody bubble spurted out his nose and he died.

What Ernie didn't know is that this relatively quick death beat the hell out of the death that was awaiting him after drinking the toxic mixture of hog runoff and enriched field byproducts combined with a lethal dose of insecticide. His body had already begun to change and Ernie would've suffered a painful death lasting a few days before he would've succumbed. So in reality, getting trashed and smashed was a good thing.

Sonny, on the other hand, wasn't as lucky. He had barely kept control of his convertible after rolling over top of Ernie. His expensive, low profile tires had taken a helluva hit, both of them blowing out on the passenger side. He swerved over the line a couple of times before getting the car in the correct lane and around another curve. He could hear the *fwap, fwap, fwap* of the tires and feel the car leaning to the right as it pulled sharply towards the ditch. He slammed on the brakes and cut to the right. He thought for a brief second that the car was going to flip and roll. *With my luck,* he thought, *I'll go over the fucking side and all they'll find is the steering wheel and my left testicle.*

The car slid, showering the scenery with a shrapnel blast of gravel, large rocks and turf slung into the darkness. The flat tires ripped free. One flew into the woods while the other lodged beneath the car. An owl looked on from the safety of a branch high above. The bird showed very little interest as the expensive wheels bounced on pavement and bounded through the rough ditch, destroying them.

Once the vehicle came to a stop and the dust had cleared, Sonny raised his bleeding head and looked around. The hood of the car was facing the centerline and the rear dropped off into the ditch. He wasn't certain how much of his dazed state was due to the wreck versus the alcohol. He had at least been wearing his seatbelt, saving him from possibly being tossed out of the ragtop. Which was unfortunate in the realm of events to come.

Sonny's mind was foggy and his vision blurred. He was trying to get his bearings as a light breeze blew, sending a waft of dead carcass his way.

"Holy shit," Sonny said, retching at the smell. His eyes opened wider and his mouth clamped shut as he threw his hand across his face in a failed attempt to block the offal.

He pushed open the broken door, which swung outward a third of the way before scraping the asphalt on the shoulderless road. He released the belt and hauled himself out of the car, which wasn't easy considering the damage and the angle that the low-lying car rested. If it hadn't been for the tires on the driver's side still being inflated, along with the one tire lodged beneath, near the oil pan, the sports car would've been sitting on its frame and probably would've caused enough sparks to start a forest fire.

He staggered around to the front of his ruined ride and looked at the remains. He searched for his cell phone but came up empty, not that he really thought he could get a signal out here. He bent down on one knee, nearly tipping over as his tequila offered to return for another round with a burning vurp. He looked at the bumper where he first heard the armadillo hit. He couldn't get his hand under much of it, but a portion was sticking up in the air. He found something slimy and sniffed his fingers. He could tell it was fleshy and maybe a little bloody. He wiped it off on the grass.

He walked around to the passenger side and tried to view the damage. It was too dark to see much but he could tell that something was sticking from beneath the car, propping it up a little. He reached underneath and found what he was searching for. He rubbed it and quickly snatched his hand back.

"Ow! Fuck!"

He had sliced his fingers open on the protruding steel of the ruined tire, his blood mingling with the fresh blood from Ernie—the infected, contagious, fresh blood.

Sonny wandered down the road in the direction he had been driving, figuring he was still another ten miles from the nearest little hick town and knew well enough that not a damn thing would be open. With any luck, he hoped to see a house with a light on, maybe some farmer getting around to go milk his cows.

He stumbled up the ditch, tripping and landing hard at an awkward angle. He heard a snap and felt a sharp pain.

"Goddamn, motherfucking, cocksucking, son-of-a-bitch!"

He couldn't really see his hand that he had just sliced on the tire, but he knew it was probably broken as he cradled it to his chest. He screamed out in pain and frustration, kicking as he rolled about and shoving his sandal through a headlight. It took him a couple of attempts to get off the ground, his hand and wrist throbbing and his foot and ankle now covered in abrasions. He stood beside the ruined car and felt around the dash, finding the latch and reaching into the glove compartment. He pulled a pint of vodka free, sticking it in the crook of his elbow so he could unscrew the cap with his one good hand and tossing it in the ditch. He took a couple of huge swigs and began walking, only making it three steps before realizing the jarring effect of walking was causing his wrist to ache more. He took a longer swig as he walked, his head tossed back while he searched the bleak loneliness of the night sky. Thousands of stars were visible, yet those little pinpoints of light twinkled too far away to do Jack shit for Sonny.

He was paying very little attention to where he ambled, heading towards the other side of the road. He was happy being oblivious after the shitaster that was tonight. He took one whoopsie-do of a step and rolled, tumbled and cartwheeled over two hundred feet down a steep, rocky slope. He was too busy yelling and hearing his body crash into trees, boulders and through bushes to notice all the snapping sounds his body was now making.

He came to rest, dangling on a shelf ledge overlooking another drop of nearly five hundred feet to dilapidated buildings and abandoned rides. But Sonny was unconscious and, unfortunately for him, still breathing. Ernie had gotten off easy. Sonny was F-U-C-T, fucked.

"Look at all the beautiful colors," Lisa said as she viewed the menagerie of autumn leaves on display. "This time of year is my favorite season."

"Enjoy the trees while you can," Darrin said. "We're close to the turnoff. Soon, you'll be crawling, squirming, climbing and wriggling through passages in a live cave."

A slight tremor went through Lisa and the hair on her arms stood up. She was both excited and a bit nervous about exploring a wild cave. She was shaken from her reverie by another male voice.

"And I'll be right behind you, watching that tight ass wriggle and giving you a hand, or two, when you need a lift or help getting through a *tight* spot."

"Do you always have to be so goddamn perverted, Rick?" Taylor shot Rick a dirty look. She didn't care much for the burly jock, but Lisa was her best friend and they did most activities together. She hated that her friend was dating Rick the Dick, as she privately liked to refer to him, but nothing she could do could persuade her friend since third grade to dump the asshole.

"Oh, come on, Taylor. Just because Darrin would prefer to rub his hands over a smooth, milky, stalactamite..."

"Stalactite or stalagmite," Darrin corrected.

"Yeah, whatever. So since he'd rather rub down a dripping cave ornament down instead of your bumps, don't get all feminist and jealous."

"Fuck you, Rick."

"Okay, okay, everyone calm down," Darrin said. "We're here to have fun. "First of all, I'd never touch a live piece of the cave, at least not with my bare hand. The oils from human skin can kill the areas you touch, messing up the environment, ecosystem and ruining the cave.

"Second, just because Taylor doesn't like you being so openly suggestive doesn't make her a feminist."

"I am a feminist."

"But even if she is, it doesn't mean you should be stepping on her freedom of speech or thoughts. Let's all just get along. We're going to be here a couple of days and we should enjoy the natural beauty of everything around us."

"Yeah, like Lisa's ass," Rick said with a laugh as he pinched the side of her thigh as best he could through her tight jeans.

Lisa playfully slapped at his hand. "Stop it or you won't be getting any for the rest of the month. And today's only the seventh."

"Shit, that's like three weeks without any nookie," Rick said as he used his fingers and looked at the ceiling of the Jeep, trying to do the math.

"I'd hand you some lotion but I'm out. How about some sandpaper and alcohol?" Taylor asked with a smirk.

"Very funny."

"It's fine grit—for getting those sensitive, little jobs done," she said with a smile. Rick didn't find that funny. Darrin and Lisa were howling with laughter.

"Awww, did my baby get his feelings hurt," Lisa asked, pouting her lips before putting her head on his shoulder and her hand on his crotch. She patted his bulge and said, "Just behave yourself. We'll see what happens in *dark caves*."

Rick smiled, knowing he was forgiven. Then he opened his mouth once again. "At least we know that cave hasn't been so abandoned it has bats in it like some caves."

Taylor reached for the flashlight in the glove compartment, a hefty metal one that held four "C" cell batteries. She had fire in her eyes. Darrin knew what she was going for and gently grabbed her wrist. She stopped and looked at him. He shook his head and mouthed, "Don't do it." She huffed but gave in.

"At least if we meet any cavemen in there I won't be mistaken for a Cro-Magnon like some of our party," she mumbled.

Rick heard her say something but couldn't quite make out what she said and wouldn't have known what it meant if he had. Darrin did hear her and suppressed a laugh.

"Speaking of abandoned caves, have any of you seen *The Descent*?" Rick asked.

Rick slapped the back of the driver's seat so hard he thrust Darrin forward enough to lock his seatbelt. He blurted out, "Dude, that movie fucking rocks."

This time Taylor looked at Darrin and shook her head, mouthing "No." He gave her a questioning look. But it was too late, for Rick was expounding in great detail the horrific scenes of the claustrophobia-inducing film. He went into great detail about what the subterranean creatures looked like, how they killed the women and the fact that their friend had purposely taken them to the wrong cave, so no one knew where they were.

Taylor turned to the back seat and could see the terror in Lisa's eyes, her face ashen white. Lisa wasn't a fan of horror films and it was all they could do to talk her into coming on this adventure. Now Lisa's boyfriend was freaking her the fuck out.

"Rick!" Taylor yelled. He shut up long enough to look at his nemesis and saw her eyes roll to his right. He turned and looked at Lisa, her fingernails digging into her pants legs and her body shaking uncontrollably.

"What's wrong, baby?"

Lisa didn't respond. She didn't even look at him when he spoke. Her eyes were glued to the back of Taylor's headrest.

Darrin couldn't really turn to see what was going on. He only caught a glimpse of Lisa in his rearview mirror, keeping an eye on her more than the highway, trying to determine if he needed to pull over before she had a meltdown.

He interjected, "Don't worry, Lisa. This place requires a permit, which I have, so the owner knows we're here this weekend. Quite a few people have gone through this cave and mapped out several miles of paths and tunnels. There are no dangerous animals."

"What about bears or cougars?" Rick asked.

Lisa let out a little yelp. Taylor turned and went for the flashlight once more.

"I'm gonna brain the asshole."

Darrin said, "Don't do it. We need that light. Just remember your training."

Taylor growled. She knew Darrin was referring to her meditation and Tai Chi. She didn't give a shit. She grabbed the half-eaten donut she had been chewing on and threw it in Rick's face before turning back and staring at the road.

"What the fuck?"

"Rick, Lisa doesn't dig scary movies," Darrin replied. "It took a lot to convince her to come on this trip. We've been planning it for most of the year."

"How was I supposed to know? We've only been dating a couple of months."

"If you'd actually talk about something besides your dick, you dumb fuck," Taylor yelled.

"What Taylor means is that you're relatively new to things and probably wasn't aware of—well, just take it easy and try and be supportive."

Rick looked at Darrin, trying not to laugh. He felt as though he was in some pansy support group. He caught the nasty look

Taylor was giving him and decided not to let her walk behind him in the cave for fear of a knife in the back. Then he turned and saw Lisa still freaked out, her eyes filled with tears and her lips trembling. It finally dawned on him that they were serious and that he had unwittingly scared his girlfriend.

"Hey, look, babe, I'm sorry. I didn't know." He caressed her hand in as calm a manner as his rough, calloused hands could manage.

He wasn't used to being sensitive. He was tough as nails, but the sensitive shit was what secretly scared Rick. So trying to be polite and gentle was unfamiliar territory for the large, defensive end of the college team. It was already a bit unsettling that Lisa was a foot shorter than him and weighed all of 110 soaking wet. He was very protective of her around his other football buddies but he was frightened of hurting her. He never could come when on top, only from behind or with her riding him, for fear of squashing her. Lisa was what Rick called a "topper." With her slight yet sexy frame, she was small enough he could just sit her on top of his cock and spin her like a top—or so he imagined.

"Come on, Leez, ain't nothing gonna hurt you. There ain't nothing in the woods bigger or badder than me."

"Or dumber," Taylor mumbled as she stared out the passenger window and tried to calm down.

"Hell, I'll wrestle a bear naked for you if you'd like," Rick said with a smile, pulling his shirt up to his neck. Like most players, he didn't have a svelte six-pack. It was a lot of blubber hanging over his belt loops because no amount of weightlifting could stave off three greasy cheeseburgers on a daily basis.

"Sounds like you'd like it," Taylor said with venom.

Rick chose to ignore Taylor's snarky remark this time, not taking his eyes off Lisa. Her color was beginning to return and she had loosened her fingers and wasn't quite digging into her legs any longer. Rick pulled her close as he scooted over to meet her halfway since she was buckled in and he had chosen not to use his seatbelt. He leaned her head against his shoulder, her straw-blonde hair falling across his chest. He kissed her on top of the head and gently squeezed her as much as he felt was safe without breaking her in two.

Lisa relaxed a little and let herself be comforted. She was aware that Rick wasn't much for communicating and learning (or remembering) things she told him. She also knew that Darrin didn't know deep down why she was terrified of tight, dark places and scary movies or books.

Taylor knew. Taylor met Lisa right after Lisa moved to Marshall in the middle of their third-grade year. Lisa had missed the first half of the school year, living in another town, going through therapy and being tutored. Her father had decided a new start was needed for both of them once Lisa was well enough. She was recovering from the horror of seeing her mother raped and mutilated. Little Lisa had cracked the lid to the trunk her mother had hidden her seven-year-old daughter in the moment she heard the glass of the kitchen door shatter across the marble-tile floor.

The blood, the brutality and her mother's death had been bad enough, but when the two intruders heard the child gasp and saw the trunk lid lifted a quarter-inch, they thought it would be funny to turn over the dresser and let the weight of it hold the trunk lid down. She was imprisoned inside the lightless cedar trunk with very little room amongst the homemade quilts. She screamed and screamed, using up her oxygen. She could hear the muffled sounds of the men going through her parent's belongings and then nothing at all beyond her own breathing and crying. The men had left the bedroom to search the rest of the house.

She banged on the lid and screamed to get out, getting on her back like a turtle flipped upside down. She used her hands and feet to try and force the lid open but the dresser was too heavy for the small girl.

One of the men came back in and slapped the trunk several times as he laughed and yelled out something about going to sleep. Then she was left alone, eventually passing out.

She didn't know how long it was before her father made it home and found her after walking in to the horror that was beyond description, for he still dearly loved his wife. Lisa awoke in a hospital bed, her hands wrapped from where she had clawed at the lid until her fingernails had torn and bled. She saw her father sitting in a chair next to her, staring blankly at the generic, white wall, tears streaming down his cheeks and his hands clasped tightly.

When she tried to speak she found that she was hoarse from screaming and had very little voice to get his attention, but he heard her. He held her in his arms for what seemed like forever, both of them crying until they fell asleep on the hospital bed, Lisa curled up in a fetal position against her father and he held her tightly, afraid to let her go.

The intruders—killers—had stolen her mom's car. A raid on a chop shop two days later accidentally turned up the car. When the district attorney told those arrested that they would be accessories to murder, they dropped dime on the two men who had brought in the car. Julio Martinez and Zander Strickland were found within the hour and hauled in with no chance for bail.

It would be nearly two years before the trial went to court and both men would be found guilty of several crimes, enough to get them both the chamber. Ten-year-old Lisa stood beside her father, tears welling in hate-filled eyes as she watched both men die on separate nights.

Ten years later she still hated brutal acts of violence, tight spaces and total darkness. Which is why she was perfectly fucked up in the head enough to be majoring in psychology, because it takes someone with a few toys in the attic to understand the broken toys in someone else's attic.

It took the summer break between third and fourth grade before she even revealed to Taylor her mom had been killed. Taylor just figured that Lisa's parents had been divorced and, in an unusual turn of events, Lisa was awarded to her dad instead of her mom.

It wasn't until junior high before she told her what she remembered of that afternoon. Taylor never repeated a word of it to anyone, not even Darrin whom she had been dating for nearly two years. Lisa had never asked Taylor not to repeat it. Taylor just knew that friends didn't repeat shit like that and that if Lisa wanted anyone else to know she would tell them. To this day, Taylor was the only person Lisa had confided in as far as she knew.

Like Rick, Taylor was protective of her best friend, against the world, not just jocks. Some charged her with being a feminist, which she was fine with. Some thought they two were lipstick lesbos, which they weren't. Lisa was the sister Taylor never had and she'd be damned if some idiot screwed with Lisa. She'd literally fight tooth and nail for her friend, having proven it a couple of times during their freshmen year. Taylor gained a reputation for being one tough bitch when she knocked out Eric Clayborne's tooth after he got a little handsy with Lisa, cornering her at her locker one afternoon after school. Taylor followed up with a knee to his balls and a hammer fist between the shoulder blades as he bent over to clutch his nuts, dropping him like a ton of potatoes in front of a dozen witnesses.

When the principal questioned each of them, he had no choice but to suspend Taylor for three days, just to show that he was trying to be unbiased. In reality, he felt she was fully in her rights and applauded her, but he couldn't publicly admit that.

Eric was expelled. He was lucky that Lisa and her father hadn't decided to press charges. The boy had felt her up enough that he probably could've gotten thrown into juvie for assault and been placed on a sex offender list.

Eric's parents considered pressing charges against Taylor until they discovered the truth of what he had done and decided they were thankful Lisa wasn't having him arrested.

After that, no one fucked with either girl, but behind their backs the rumors of being carpet munchers increased. So Lisa made an effort to date the hottest guys in school. Not because she gave a damn what they said about her. She had survived true atrocities and being called a lesbian wasn't shit to her. But she hated they said stuff about her best friend, who wasn't a drop-dead beauty, but she was attractive, funny, intelligent and loyal. So going overboard dating the jocks to derail the rumors was Lisa's way to try and help Taylor, who never had a real boyfriend until her senior year. That was Darrin. Lisa liked him and approved, so their trio was nigh inseparable.

It took many evenings of discussion and a lot of wine to get Lisa to agree to this trip. But Darrin had some photos he had found online of the wild cave that others had posted. Plus, she knew he had been spelunking for half his life with his father and uncle. He was a responsible person, had a steady job, was punctual, not a slob and Lisa trusted that he knew what he was doing. The thought of camping in the fall was enticing as was getting away from town, riding out in the mountains and the forest. She thought it might be possible to spot elk, deer and other wildlife (although she wasn't sure whether she wanted to see a bear or not). She had her camera and a couple of charged batteries, hoping they'd last her for the weekend excursion.

She knew Darrin was a tolerant guy and he was making do with Rick being with them. She knew that Taylor hated Rick, but she was hoping that this chance to get him away from his buddies and out in nature might show a different side of him. Then maybe her friends could find something about him they liked. But they had only been on the road for a couple of hours and Rick had just gotten out of the shower after practice, so he was still testosterone driven and hadn't chilled out. Waiting on him also threw them behind three hours later than Darrin had originally planned. She knew Darrin wouldn't be mad at her, but she felt guilty.

She knew Rick wasn't trying to be mean or scare her. At least he was trying to make up for his mistake instead of teasing her about it. She snuggled up to him. Rick stayed quiet for once, which was the right thing to do whether he knew it or not. His silence was simply because he wasn't sure what to say and he didn't want to add one more fuck up to his long list he had acquired just in the past couple of hours.

Darrin cranked up the radio but only received an earful of static, the remote locale and mountains making it impossible to get a signal. He switched it over to the new Halestorm disc, a combination of hard rock and power ballads that could cross over from rock to the country charts. Darrin dug the band, and singer Lzzy Hale, but figured that the mixture of song styles would have something that everyone would like, even if it were only one or two songs here and there. Darrin loved everything the band had put out. He tried not to let on how much of a crush he had on the singer/guitarist, but Taylor knew. She figured it was innocent enough and didn't say anything. She had no worries Darrin would ever meet the singer and leave her to hit the road as a male groupie.

At the moment he was just hoping to fill the void and clear some of the air in the Jeep. He felt bad for Lisa, and he was glad that Taylor was strapped into the front seat or he would be pulling her off of Rick like a wildcat attacking a grizzly.

And he knew Rick was clueless. For Lisa's sake he was trying very hard to get along with the jock, attempting to be tolerant of his ignorance and obviously low intelligence. Darrin did notice that Rick did his best to protect Lisa and treated her like a China doll, which is why he was making an effort to like Rick. The guy might be a doofus but he would take care of Lisa as long as their love remained. So maybe it was a good thing because he knew that for some reason his good friend needed the strong, protective type in her life. Now that she wasn't living at home and near her dad, she relied on a substitute. Darrin didn't know psychology, but he figured that if large, protective lugs calmed her and helped her function then it was a good thing.

As Lisa calmed, Darrin slowed and looked at a road sign so shot up as a target for the locals that it was difficult to read. He turned left, getting off the main highway and coming to a stop.

"Taylor, check out the map, please. I believe this is where

we're supposed to turn."

Taylor pulled the map from beneath the flashlight she had so wanted to utilize. She opened it and spent a moment getting her bearings, finally finding where she thought they were. Meanwhile, Darrin was attempting to use his phone to do the same thing but couldn't get a signal. For all his app knew, he was in Abu Dhabi.

Taylor looked up at the sign, back at the map and up at the damaged sign once again. "I don't think this is it, but it's hard to tell since the yokels have been using that as target practice," she said, gesturing with her head to the sign. "It could be County Road 83, but with the bottom mostly missing that could be an eight or a two instead of a three."

"Dude, it's an adventure. Take it."

Darrin paused, chewing over what Rick was suggesting. He stared at the bullet-riddled sign.

"I know we're in the general area," he said. "This probably is the right turnoff. There should be a place three or four miles up the road to pull over and a hiking trail that leads to the cave mouth."

Darrin continued onwards, up the mystery road. The road was rough and rocky. A little over four miles along the dusty path a cleared area that looked as if used as a pullover was apparent. Across from the parking spot was a path a little grown over and not much wider than a typical deer trail.

"We're here," said Darrin. He attempted to exude confidence in his statement. In reality, he wasn't too certain. The location seemed similar to the directions he had written down but everything was just a little off. Then again, the old timer who owned the property had provided directions with descriptions such as, "...just keep going 'til you get to the ol' oak Jesse Turner hit that time he had gotten some bad shine and started goin' blind, right there in the middle of the dadgum road. Bought that radiator fluid off of Homer Jenkins who disappeared not long after that. Some say the families of his blind or dead customers ran him off. Others say he got et by bigfoot. Anywho, it drove Jesse's engine block all the way to the bed of the pickemup, taking Jesse with it, pinning him to the tailgate.

"Then you'll hang a left onto 83 and go a ways, pro'lly three, maybe four or five miles 'til you get to a patch of grass on the right and a trail on the left. Follow the trail a half hour or so and you'll see a big ol' hole in the earth. Big enough to swallow a herd of elk and dark as a black bear's asshole. Should be some blackberry bushes in bloom 'round the area and a sign from Uncle Sam saying it's private property and a permit is required. It's my property but to prevent being sued if'n people got hurt I registered it with the officials so anyone goin' in without permission wasn't my responsibility. Of course, someone wanting to throw a lawsuit at me might find themselves on the wrong end of a double barrel in the middle of the night."

Darrin surveyed the landscape and saw blackberry bushes everywhere, just like the entire trip up the dirt road. The white petals stood out amongst the background of colorful fall leaves covering the ground, a few red, yellow and orange leaves still clinging to tree limbs. Taylor interrupted his thoughts.

"Are you sure? That trail looks like it hasn't been used by a person anytime recently."

Darrin countered, "Well, it's not like that many people come up here to go spelunking, and it was a wet September, so the trail's going to be a little wild."

"Bro, we're going to need a machete," said Rick.

Darrin cringed at being called bro but bit his tongue and said nothing. He opened the door and made his way around to the back, opening it and began to dig through the packs to pull his own supplies and equipment—along with a machete. He sliced downwards through the air as he strode to the beginning of the trail, looking it over while waiting for the others to grab their backpacks, ropes, helmets and gloves. Normally he would assist everyone, making certain their headlamps on their hardhats worked and they had everything they would need. He had double and triple checked each pack before loading them into the Jeep, but he typically checked once more in case something rattled loose or a bulb broke on the rough trip. But Darrin's mind was pre-occupied with doubt about whether they were at the right location or not.

He soon felt Taylor's touch his shoulder. He reached a hand up to encompass her hand. He could hear Rick and Lisa closing the back of the Jeep. He pulled his keys from his pocket and locked the door remotely.

"What's going on? You seem like you're in your own little world."

Darrin looked at Taylor, her question just beginning to register. He looked at the other couple then back at the path.

"I don't know. Something just seems off, but maybe I'm just being a little paranoid taking two newbies and one of them being claustrophobic."

"I don't really know if what you call Lisa's problem claustrophobia. I think it's more a fear of stressful and brutal situations," Taylor said, once more backing her friend. "She'll be fine. As long as Rick doesn't open his mouth she'll look to him as a protector, in addition to me sticking close to her." She hugged Darrin and gave him a kiss on the cheek. He reciprocated and let himself relax a little.

"Hey, hey! So going into a cave was all code for coming out here in the wild and getting down, huh?"

Darrin and Taylor turned, both giving a scowl at Rick as he approached with his arms held out wide and a huge smile on his face. His backpack was dangling by its strap from one of his large, muscular arms.

"No, Rick, we're actually here to go spelunking," Darrin said emphatically. "So just put your hormones in park and be our rear guard as we hike the trail to the cave entrance.

"Lisa, why don't you walk between Rick and Taylor? The trail shouldn't be too difficult. We'll get to the mouth, take a break, and then head in. We should be there in half an hour or so."

"Yeah, babe," Rick said with a lascivious grin. "I'll watch your rear all the way until I go in the dark hole."

He swatted her playfully on the ass. Lisa wasn't in the mood and brushed at Rick's hand still clutching her right buttcheek.

Taylor was ripping her rock pick free of her pack, a storm brewing in her eyes as she swung around to face the football player. Darrin grabbed her wrist and held her tight to prevent Rick's murder.

The hike was going well with Rick occasionally saying something that required no response from the others and Lisa enjoying the relaxing moments in between as she took nature photos now and then. She even managed to get Taylor to pose for a couple of shots next to colorfully adorned trees.

Once Darrin realized they had been hiking for forty-five minutes, he put it down to pausing for picture taking. Once they had been traveling for an hour and saw no end of the trail or a cave, he began to worry. He lied to himself, telling himself every minute that their destination was just around the next tree or bend.

He also noticed a lack of wildlife. Granted, most animals are going to run off when they sense four humans, but surely there should be some birds or insects. It was still early in the season and hadn't gotten that cold yet.

Scooting up beside her boyfriend, Taylor said, "We've been on this quasi-trail quite a while. Are you sure you heard the guy correctly on the directions?"

"As correctly as possible with his descriptive manner of details that matter to no one except some Billy Bob who's lived here his entire life."

The frustration in Darrin's answer was obvious. He was about to suggest they turn back when they rounded a large ball root from a fallen hickory tree. The other trees beyond it thinned and the path widened before a clearing. Past the clearing was a rotting cedar split-rail fence, a portion of the stack knocked over just a few yards from the back of a weathered, wood plank building with a collapsing cedar shingled roof.

"Whoa, what's this place?" Rick asked as he looked around at the multiple weathered buildings, battered signs and ancient rides that looked as though they hadn't been operated in a couple of decades. Rust was more evident than paint and some rides had parts dangling haphazardly. A miniature train sat forlorn upon a weed-infested track that looked as if it encircled the park.

"I think we're at the old Wildwood theme park," Lisa said. My parents said they used to come here a lot as teens back when they were dating but it closed down about the time I was born. It was a hillbilly/mountain man park based on the way this region sort of looked around the late 19th century."

"We're not in the right place," Darrin said, disbelief coming from the disheartened biology major. His shoulders sagged. Taylor grabbed his hand and held it tight. He looked at her and said, "We're on the wrong side of the highway. We probably should've turned right another mile or so down from that damn sign all shot to hell."

Taylor smiled, trying to cheer Darrin up. "So we'll rest here for a bit, have some lunch and check the place out then we'll cross the highway and walk down it until we get back to the sign. We can stuff our packs somewhere to make better time and then drive back and get them before we go to the correct turnoff."

"We'll be behind a day," Darrin said, still angry with himself. "I knew something wasn't right."

"No worries," Taylor said. "So we won't get to explore as much of the cave. We can camp out tonight by the cave and hit it first thing in the morning."

"Yeah, bro. Not a cloud in the sky," Rick said, looking up from a kiss with Lisa. "We'll make some s'mores, roast a pack of hot dogs, tell ghost stories..."

Taylor shot Rick a dirty look. He tried to correct his mistake.

"Like about Casper and Scooby Doo type ghost shit, ya know. Nothing scary or anything like that."

Lisa looked up at Rick as he tried to extract his foot from his mouth. She smacked him on the chest and giggled.

"You are such a doofus," she said. She went over to Darrin and looked him in his downcast eyes. She was four inches shorter, so looking up into the hazel of his eyes wasn't difficult.

"Hey, it's all good. We have no set agenda. I know you wanted to be in the cave two days. But we're here to just relax and have fun, right? Right?" she asked again, shaking him lightly when he didn't respond.

He gave her a smile and answered, "Yeah, you're right. We'll make it work."

Lisa grabbed Darrin's free hand. She and Taylor marched him forward, playfully swinging their arms like little kids, forcing their sullen leader to join in. The building had been a shop where they had demonstrated how the old timers made lye soap. They sold what they made to the park visitors according to the sign hanging precariously by a remaining, rusty chain. Lisa imagined women in gingham or calico dresses standing in front of a large, black kettle with a wood fire stoked beneath as they stirred an odorous liquid with a paddle. She had once seen photos of her great-grandmother making soap.

"I wonder if it still smells like soap in the shop?" Lisa said, pulling Darrin and Taylor along as she went to the front door.

Rick wasn't into girly stuff like soap, but he followed the trio only to find them covering their noses and mouths. "Holy hell, this smells worse than Aaron Sarkowski's locker."

"Isn't he that guy who wears the same socks all season long for good luck?" Darrin asked with a muffled voice, his hand still in place over the lower portion of his face.

"Yeah, and he feels the same about his underwear and jock strap."

Both girls gagged and were visibly appalled by the thought as they turned from the empty, dust-coated shelves and looked at one another. They all exited the abandoned shop and took great gulps of air.

"It smells like something died in there," Taylor said.

"Like multiple things," Darrin added. "But I didn't see a carcass or any signs of maggots and the various other bugs that feed on the dead."

"Darrin, please," Taylor said, placing a hand in the air and motioning for him to stop describing.

"Sorry, but it's all just part of my major. I did notice something had disturbed the dust on the floor. It looked like a footprint beside another print, like maybe a foot being dragged."

"Ha, ha. Now who's trying to creep everyone out?" Rick asked. He noticed no one else was laughing.

"What? I thought he was just trying to freak you girls out."

"No, I was serious. The prints weren't fresh. There was a thin layer of dust on them, but someone has been here recently."

"Probably just some curious trespassers," Taylor said.

"Yeah," Rick laughed. "Like us."

"Let's check out some of the other buildings," Darrin suggested. "Maybe there's a pavilion or an intact table where we can eat lunch."

"Yeah, between practice and that hike through the middle of nowhere, I'm starved."

"Why doesn't that surprise us, Rick?" Taylor said with disdain.

Lisa moved closer to her boyfriend. It was still daylight but Darrin's observation had worried her. They walked past a glass blower's shop and furnace next door to the "Whittlin' House." Rick found a rusty knife shoved between a brace and the wall. The blade was only three inches long and the grip was half-rotted away, but he shoved it into the space between his belt and beltloop at the back of his right hip, just behind the large scabbard holding his Bowie knife.

They passed a couple of kiddie rides, some small swings that went around in a circle with a totem pole post carved like a giant bear and a merry-go-round that had horses along with carved bears, cougars and deer.

Darrin stepped up on the carousel, admiring the craftsmanship. "Man, these are cool. These antique figures go for a fortune on those reality shows. Look at the detail."

"Cool, let's take a couple when we come back with the Jeep," Rick said. It was difficult to tell if he was joking or not, so no one answered him.

"This one has a little too much detail," Taylor said. She pointed to the muzzle of a ferocious looking bear, its lips drawn back in a carved smile but the remnants of dark red blood was still evident. It looked as though something had recently left the mark. Darrin looked down and saw blood drops spilled in the dusty platform leading between the other carousel figures. "Hmmm... the same footprints, one normal and one dragging as if someone was injured."

Taylor could see Lisa was beginning to tense up as she stared at the evidence. She casually suggested, "Maybe someone had been out here messing around, got hurt and simply tried to find some shelter until help arrived. Even these prints are covered in a layer of dust. Whoever it was is probably at home with their leg propped on a pillow while they watch reruns and feed their face."

Rick held up his index finger, as if a light bulb had popped on in his head. "Or they..."

Lisa turned around, fear in her eyes as she anticipated the suggestion Rick was about to make. He too realized he was about to do it again.

"Or they, injured their foot and not their leg. Right, Taylor?"

Lisa couldn't see Taylor behind her shaking her long, brown curls in disbelief at Rick's stupidity.

"Sure thing—a leg or foot injury," Darrin said, filling in the awkward silence. "Look, there's a couple of picnic tables over there next to that little food shack. It's overlooking a pond. That should be relaxing."

The group made their way across the grounds, going to the table nearest the pond until they took a whiff of the putrid water and saw all the scum floating across the top. They decided on the table furthest from the pond, giving them a little shade beneath an elm as they pulled their packs off their backs and got comfy.

"That feels much better," Taylor said, stating the obvious. "Give me a moment and I'll pull the peanut butter and jelly sandwiches out. I think Lisa might have the chips in her pack."

Lisa had been staring intently at the pond. Something about the nasty water gave her the willies but she wasn't sure why. She heard her name mentioned and asked what. Taylor repeated her statement and Lisa acknowledged she had the chips, going to work on opening her pack to distract her from the pond.

Darrin was keeping up with what was going on, but he was also still thinking about the lack of wildlife. Even a water source as foul as this acre-sized pool of muck should've had some insects buzzing around or floating on the surface. Something just wasn't right.

They ate their lunch, discussing upcoming exams, but Darrin surreptitiously kept an eye peeled for any sign of danger. It was past two, which gave them maybe three more hours of light depending on how quickly the sun dipped down behind the mountain peaks. It was going to be a close call making it back to the Jeep and finding the road they were supposed to turn on before darkness fell. The moon would be close to half full tonight, if the clouds that were beginning to move in didn't hang around. But he wasn't sure if they would make it to the cave or just have to sleep at the trailhead.

They finished lunch and repacked their stuff, making sure to pack their trash in a small trash bag and take it with them. They made their way around the pond where a small pier led out over the water. The faded sign had a picture of a happy catfish being caught with a cane pole by a sleeping, barefoot hillbilly in overalls, complete with straw hat, corncob pipe and a can labeled "wurms" beside him. Instructions followed describing that the kid's pond was for ages 16 and under and the kids got to keep what they caught, the fish being prepared and packed on ice at a little fishing shack off to the side.

"Man, this place must've been awesome when it was in full swing," Rick said. "I would've loved coming to a park like this." He walked out on the pier surrounded on each side by thick stands of cattails almost as tall as he was, the bottoms of the plants hidden by the muck and dirty water.

He was near the very end, only thirty or forty feet from the others, when his foot crashed through a rotten board. He dropped, one leg sinking into the water and the rest of him still on the wooden pier. He let out a painful scream, wincing as he grasped at his leg.

"Rick," Lisa screamed. She started to run out to him but Darrin placed his arm in front of her.

"Let me go," he suggested as he stripped his pack and set it on the ground. "That pier might break through somewhere else. You two just stay here and get out the first aid kit in my stuff."

The girls did as suggested while Darrin cautiously made his way out to Rick, who was cursing up a storm as he tried to pull his leg free. When Darrin got to him, he crouched down, testing the surrounding boards.

"My goddamn leg is hung up in something. I think there's a trap under here because something snapped down on my fucking ankle like a starved dog being thrown a steak."

"Okay, let me help. Try to keep your voice down to between us so the girls don't come rushing out here and get hurt."

Rick nodded. His eyes were filled with tears but he didn't care. Darrin decided that if the jock wasn't trying to act tough and his face was so flushed then he must really be in some major pain. He stuck his hands through the jagged hole and detestable water then followed the leg down to something metal. He felt around and recognized the feel of a steel-jaw trap.

Looking Rick in the eyes, he said, "You're right. It's a trap. Probably used to catch beavers messing up the pond or otters that were eating the fish. I'm going to have to lay on my stomach and reach down with both hands. When I pry the jaws apart try to carefully pull your leg free. If you jar my hands or smack me in the face the odds are I'll lose my grip and the trap will snap back down on you and me."

Rick nodded, beads of sweat spreading across his brow and running down his face.

"Ready?"

Rick nodded. He could see Lisa and Taylor as Darrin got prone and reached in the water with both arms extended as far as he could stretch them. The girls had bandages, scissors and alcohol ready, waiting nervously for any news.

Rick could feel Darrin trying to get a firm grip, shifting the teeth, feeling them grind and embed a little deeper into his flesh. He was certain that at least one steel tooth on each side had made it all the way to the bone. He did as he had been taught in football, trying to breathe through the pain instead of holding his breath. He could see Darrin starting to strain and felt the trap release its hold, tearing more meat from his leg as it did so.

"That's as wide as I can get it," Darrin said, grunting as his body shook with the strain. "Can you get your leg free?"

"I think so," Rick answered.

He used his hands to pull his injured limb upwards. The teeth snagged on his shoelace, threatening to slam shut with enough force to cut off his foot and Darrin's fingers in one powerful snap. He turned his foot a bit and, with extreme pain and trying not to cry out like a little bitch (or so he believed), he flexed his toes downwards and slipped his foot between the jaws.

When Darrin saw the top of Rick's shoe emerging from the water he let the trap go, quickly pulling his hands up and away. Once he had them free of the water he checked to make sure there were ten moss and algae covered digits between the two hands. He rolled over on his back and took in a deep breath, his scum-covered hands resting on his heaving chest.

"Fuck, that was intense," Darrin said in a rare display of profanity. He was still breathing hard and looking into the sky as he asked, "Still have all of your parts?"

"Yeah, but it's definitely broken and bleeding like a son-of-a-bitch."

"We've got to cut your pants leg free and get that wound cleaned now."

Darrin rolled over and got to his feet. He tested the boards close to Rick. Once he determined it could probably hold his weight he bent down and helped Rick get to his feet, the jock's arm thrown over Darrin's shoulders. Each wobbly step and hop back to land presented an opportunity to crash through the water-logged boards or to fall over into the water and cattails.

The girls were screaming for them to come on, as if it wasn't obvious. Their concern was evident, even Taylor seemed genuinely worried. As the two guys made it to the beginning of the pier, Rick's good foot caught a nail head sticking up just enough to cause the young men to stumble. They were propelled forward, crashing into the ground. Rick finally let out an anguished scream, the intensity finally overwhelming him as it sent a jolt of pain through his entire body.

Dusting himself off, Darrin ordered, "Hand me the scissors. Taylor, get the bandages and alcohol ready. Lisa, pull off his belt. We've got to make a tourniquet." Despite the gunk covering Rick's leg, he could tell there was plenty of blood and they needed to stop the flow.

Lisa was unbuckling Rick's belt. He attempted a smile, his mouth faintly moving into a grin as he said, "Damn, this wasn't the situation I dreamed about you stripping me."

She smiled back and said, "Shut up, pervert. Remember, Taylor has that alcohol in hand she promised you earlier."

Darrin began cutting away Rick's pant leg just above the knee, moving the leg enough to send another surge of pain through Rick. He passed out, going into shock.

It took the three of them a while to get the wound cleaned as best they could, wrapped and, using pieces of narrow shelves from the fishing shack, splinting his leg. Lisa tore the sleeve from her shirt and doused it with cool water to try and prevent him from succumbing to the blood loss and shock. His breathing and heart rate had remained steady enough that he didn't require CPR. He awakened a time or two, slurring his words and seemingly confused, but at least he was alive.

He now rested beneath a nearby pecan tree with his head on one of his own T-shirts. Lisa had laid Rick's windbreaker over his torso to keep him from getting chilled. She laid her own jacket over his injured leg and his feet, which were now bare to prevent his shoes from restricting him. Lisa had wanted to move him into a building, but the nearest one was 20 yards away and Darrin was afraid of risking moving and jostling him around that much when he was in shock.

"Now what do we do?" Taylor quietly asked Darrin as they sat a few feet away from the other couple. She was using most of her water from her canteen to wash the blood from her and Darrin's hands. She hated to waste the water, but she couldn't handle the blood and pond scum they were covered in.

Darrin was attempting to get a 9-1-1 call out, knowing it was a lost cause. He put his phone back in his pocket. "I think the best thing to do is you two stay here with Rick. I'll run back up the road and get the Jeep."

He could see that Taylor wasn't excited by the idea.

"Look, I know it sounds scary, but I can move faster on my own. Besides, I don't think Lisa is strong enough to stay here with Rick on her own. She needs some support."

"I know," Taylor said. "No sense in wishing there was some other alternative."

"Maybe I'll get lucky and there will be another car that can give me a lift. But it's going to get dark really soon. I need to go now."

"Make sure you got your keys, a long sleeve shirt and some water. Oh, and take the machete, just in case some strapping hill woman tries to abduct you for a shotgun wedding."

"Yes, dear," he said, smiling and giving her a kiss.

"Lisa, I'll be back as soon as I can with the Jeep. You two take care of Rick and we'll strap him over the hood like a deer when I get back. He'll like that."

Lisa tried to smile, knowing Darrin was trying to make her feel at ease. She mouthed the words "be careful" but he couldn't hear her.

He gave Taylor one more kiss, but before he left he whispered, "There's a small hatchet on the side of my pack," pointing to their packs in the shade of the pecan. "There's a flare gun near the bottom. I'll take my flashlight and you each have flashlights and the lights for your helmets."

"I know. Now haul ass and get back here as soon as you can."

Taylor watched Darrin begin jogging towards what they figured was the front of the park. She strode over to her friend and wrapped an arm around her, hugging her tight.

"We're going to get out of this. Rick will be okay, you'll see. Just may miss playing this season. He'll have to be happy with sitting on the bench and slapping his teammates on the ass as they go by."

Lisa wasn't surprised how caring Taylor was being. Even though Taylor wasn't thrilled with Rick, she had a good heart when need be.

"I'm going to gather a few more pieces of wood and some of the dry weeds over there so we can build a fire. It's going to be dark and cooling off really soon."

Lisa nodded her head and placed her hand against Rick's face, not certain if she was comforting him or herself. She watched his chest move up and down, making sure he was breathing, but she refused to look down at his blood-soaked, bandaged leg unless she had to. Every few minutes she would check his toes to make sure they weren't losing circulation and she would adjust the tourniquet.

Just as the sun was disappearing behind a tree line high upon the ridge, Taylor had managed to get the fire going, only needing a few matches to get a decent enough flame to build upon. Soon they had a nice fire which would've been perfect for the things they had planned to do tonight while camping if it hadn't been for their current situation.

Darrin had found the employee entrance and parking lot, which was much closer to the highway than if he had taken the alternate route and crossed the fairly large customer parking lot where rusty signs mentioned arrival and departure locations for the trams, the customer lot being so immense that the bus-like vehicles were used to transport people to the distant locations.

Once to the road for the park, he saw the sign for the highway and followed it, passing the entrance to the park. He stopped to catch his breath before choosing to walk a while. He headed back up the asphalt towards the highway he turned on a few hours earlier that would lead to his vehicle, only now he was further down the road, a portion untraveled. He took a drink from his canteen, tilting his head back and observing the dusky sky. He put away the water and reached for the flashlight, not turning it on just yet but wanting to have it in hand because it wouldn't be long before it was dark.

A rustling noise amongst the dead leaves alerted Darrin, whatever making the sound was quickly approaching him. He gripped the flashlight tighter, prepared to swing if needed while fumbling with the catch on his sheath for the machete. The woods here were deep in shadow. He decided to turn the flashlight on, hoping to see whatever was coming his way and also hoping that the light might temporarily blind it to give him that extra second if he needed to run or fight.

Twigs snapped and more leaves crunched. Darrin dropped his aim to the forest floor as the sounds seemed to be at the edge, approaching the ditch. A large rabbit leapt out in front of him and darted across the barren road and over the ditch on the other side. It hadn't even paused to look at the human or to see if traffic was barreling down the highway. Whatever frightened it had done a good job and the blur of brown and white disappeared in the darkness of more trees.

Darrin exhaled, letting the tension drain from him. He snapped the catch closed on the sheath, embarrassed that he was about to go all Ginsu on a bunny.

He began walking again, going around a sharp hairpin curve where a rocky shelf jutted out towards the road along with a yellow sign warning of dangerous curves and a speed limit of 15 m.p.h. The sun was finally disappearing beneath the tall trees as he stepped past the shelf.

The attack was sudden and brutal. A decrepit, human-like creature ambushed him. It smelled rotten and Darrin probably would've noticed the stench if the creature hadn't been downwind. It clutched Darrin about the throat, throttling him. It appeared to be what was once a large man with a scraggily beard if his quick judgment of the over-sized flannel shirt and overalls was any indication. Death had not been kind to the undead man. For all Darrin knew, he might have been the model many years ago for the fishing sign at the park.

He was desperately trying to pull his machete free but the chokehold and being forced down and back made it difficult for him to keep his balance, much less accomplish something with dexterity. Darrin swung the light with all his force, smashing it into the decaying head of the living corpse. Darrin was running low on oxygen, but the zombie was running low on skull and mushy brains.

With a final effort, Darrin smashed the undead being one

more time, caving in the remainder of its head. The monster's grip loosened, the gnarled hand dropping from Darrin's throat as it collapsed to the pavement. Darrin bent over, hacking and coughing. He felt the tender muscles of his damaged neck. He spit blood on the back of the dead being and raised up.

Another set of hands reached around Darrin from behind. Sonny, or what was once known as Sonny, had been what had spooked the rabbit. Now it was biting into the base of Darrin's cranium, chomping through the spinal cord, severing the cluster and began munching its way up into the biology major's cerebellum. The flashlight lens shattered and the plastic and metal pieces splintered away as the device met asphalt.

"Did he just say something?"

Lisa looked up at Taylor, the warm glow of the fire reflecting off her friend's glasses. She said, "Yeah, he muttered 'water.' I think he might be coming around."

She opened her own canteen and placed it at Rick's lips, lifting his head just a little. She tipped the canteen and managed to get him to drink. Rick even wiped his own mouth where the water had dribbled down the side.

"He's moving. Maybe he's out of the woods." She looked around at the encroaching darkness, the fire being the only light as the moon wasn't visible over the mountaintop or through the clouds, which had settled in thick and fluffy. "So to speak," she added with a slight shiver. "Do you think Darrin's okay?"

"Of course," Taylor answered. "He might appear dweebish, but he's pretty good at taking care of himself, especially in the wild. He doesn't panic. You know that. I just hope he can see well enough to make good time. I've had all the outdoors I want for the weekend. Damn the cave and camping."

Taylor's tone had changed from confidence to sounding like she was on the verge of breaking down and crying. Lisa recognized it for what it was and wished she could comfort her friend with a hug or a touch of the hand, but she wasn't going to leave Rick's side at the moment.

"Yeah, went caving," Taylor said with disgust. "Excuse me, spelunking—and ended up in Hillbilly Hell. It seems like this trip was cursed from the start."

Lisa didn't believe in omens, but she was reconsidering that belief system.

The fire crackled and popped as a couple of the boards burned all the way through and collapsed, sending a shower of sparks into the night sky. The flames were still lively, but Taylor felt it could use another plank or two to bolster it and extend the luminance radius.

"Back in a sec," she said to Lisa. "Need to find the little girl's room, or at least a building to squat behind. Be my luck your boyfriend would come to about the time I dropped my pants. I'll bring back some more wood."

"Don't go too far. Whistle or something so I know where you're at and that you're okay."

"Seriously?" Taylor asked with a laugh. "Fine," she said as she saluted Lisa and marched off, whistling "Heigh-Ho" from her favorite animated movie.

"Thank you, Dopey," Lisa called out.

"Whatever," Taylor called back as she made her way to the nearest building. "And it's Grumpy, bitch."

"Thank you, Grumpy Bitch."

Taylor turned and pointed at her buddy, "You are so going to get it. You have to sing a song when I get back. And I mean sing loud enough to wake the dead."

Lisa laughed as she put a hand to Rick's forehead. The clamminess and beads of sweat were dissipating and she could feel the warmth of the fire to the left side of his face. He wasn't burning up, but he was getting a little toasty.

Taylor crossed the cracked asphalt path sprouting small clumps of weeds. On the other side was a ride called The Spinning Jug, completely painted to look like a jug of moonshine with "XXX" across the side and a drunken hillbilly with little swirls coming from his head. A flame came out of his mouth as if he'd belched. The very top, above the observation deck, the roof resembled a giant cork.

Basically, it was a barrel ride where people entered a round room and stood against a wall, the top of the room open for observers to watch as the barrel picked up speed and the centrifugal force pinned the riders to the wall as the floor dropped about a foot beneath them. She remembered a similar ride at another park and it never failed that some asshole would tip his bag of popcorn or a drink full of some sticky beverage, splattering everyone spinning in the barrel. The unlucky recipients of the sugar bath would attract the bees and other insects the rest of the day.

Taylor had to admit that she enjoyed the speed of such rides, even if it didn't allow her to do much more than to try and turn so she could hang sideways while her long hair clung to the walls like a bizarre octopus. At the moment she was going let the force of gravity assist in draining her bladder, hopefully without getting it on her shoes and without squatting down on some weed trying to shoot up her crotch. It would be just her luck to sit on poison ivy and end up with an itchy cootchie.

She looked behind her and could see Lisa and Rick beside the fire. She still wasn't sure what her friend saw in the walking toadstool, and she wasn't sure if she should feel sorry for him obtaining such a serious injury or if she should be pissed at the idiot. After all, he was the reason they were still stuck way the fuck out in the middle of an abandoned park. She could only fathom how many black bears, bobcats, cougars and coyotes sought shelter here, just lying in wait to pounce from the shadows and eat her. Hell, that would be her luck even more so, squatting on poison ivy and being half eaten by a bear, only to be found with her pants down, her ass for the world to see and ugly poison ivy blisters all over her twat that would probably be mistaken for genital warts. Her tombstone would read, "Here lies Taylor, whose ass was bare. Saved from an STD, eaten by a bear."

"Get a grip," she muttered to herself.

She heard a call in a sing-song manner, "Oh, Dopey, I don't hear whistling."

"Eat my crack," she yelled back as she rounded the corner of the framework holding the jug.

"As you wish, Grumpy Bitch."

Taylor smiled. She missed the quieter days when it was just the two of them hanging out without the complications of guys, exams and adulthood.

She could barely see the flicker of the fire's flames this far away and there was no light coming from the backside of the ride. She swept her foot a couple of times across a patch of ground to see if she came kicked any weeds or trash. The area seemingly clear, she unzipped her pants and pulled them and her panties all the way to the tops of her hiking boots. She placed her ass to the wall after she squatted down, using the Jug for support. She felt her foot rub up against something solid and timidly reached down. She discovered a coil of thick rope, probably used for a swinging rope bridge support. It was grungy and possibly rotted but she couldn't really tell in the darkness. Despite the cold, her imagination was running wild and the thoughts of snakes or rats coming out of the pile ran rampant.

It took her a moment before she could relax enough to let the stream start flowing. She was hunched forward enough to miss her clothes as she returned to whistling a lively rendition of "Zip-a-Dee-Doo-Dah." Steam arose from the asphalt, the temperature having dropped enough. Taylor didn't doubt it because her ass and legs were freezing and she had goose bumps all across her thighs.

She was almost finished and reached in a pocket while trying not to tumble over into her own pool of piss.

"Fuck, I left the toilet paper in my backpack." She wiggled her butt a little to try and shake any residue free and sighed as she stood up.

Lisa listened to Taylor's whistling, noticing a pause in the tune and an unintelligible rant. Taylor had no compunction about stating what was on her mind and told anyone, including Lisa, whatever she felt needed saying. Lisa figured her friend was just bitching about the cold, the darkness, their situation or the world in general. She was used to Taylor's rants.

Then she heard a terrifying scream. The outburst was loud enough that even Rick stirred and his eyes opened halfway to see Lisa jumping up from beside him. He couldn't figure out why there was a fire in her bedroom and the power must be out because one side of him felt a chill.

"Taylor? Taylor?" Lisa was screaming at the top of her lungs, moving a few steps away from the fire and towards where she last saw her friend.

A hand clutching her jeans, which were pulled up to her mound of Venus and leaving her muscular ass still hanging out, Taylor looked like some of the idiots who wore their pants down to their knees like they had last week's doo weighing their pants down and were too stupid to buy a belt. The difference being they held the fly of their pants with a thumb and forefinger, like they had a pecker only an inch long. Taylor's fist gripped the front of her pants as she tried to hike the backside up higher with her other hand. If not for modesty's sake then she was attempting to get them in place for the sake of getting some distance between her and whoever was following her from behind The Spinning Jug.

"Taylor?" Lisa yelled again as she pointed behind her at the figure lurching out of the darkness.

Trying to catch her breath, lifting her pants, which were now halfway covering her rump, and running was taking a toll on Taylor as she tried not to stumble and take a header onto the broken path. She yelled, gasping, "Get Rick and run!"

Panicked, Lisa looked at Rick, who was trying to shake the cobwebs from his head. She looked back at Taylor who was now almost upon her. The anonymous figure was still a few yards behind. She noticed that not only were his movements hampered, but his body was contorted in a strange manner and he seemed to be missing a hand the best she could tell. She didn't want to wait for him to get closer to confirm.

"Rick's in no condition to run," she yelled back, despite Taylor now only three strides away.

Taylor rushed into her friend's waving arms, using her to steady herself as she hurriedly pulled her jeans up the remainder of the way. She was simultaneously trying to drive Lisa back just with the force of her own body pressed up against her.

"Sounds crazy, but I think it's a fucking zombie," Taylor said, the words exploding out of her mouth so fast that Lisa thought she misunderstood her at first.

Then the one-handed creature came more into the light. His pants were shredded and his "Hold my Beer—Watch this!" T-shirt was disheveled and splotched with blood. Part of his face appeared to be worm-ridden amongst the missing chunks of muscles and skin that once covered his cheek and around his eye. Moaning and with his jaw dropping open, overextending like a snake swallowing its prey since most of the muscles to hold it in place were non-existent, the zombie began reaching for them. He was still a few feet away.

"Do you think he can understand us?" Taylor asked.

"Are you going to negotiate with him? Who cares?"

"I'm hoping he doesn't understand when I tell you to get over there and try to move Rick behind the tree and out of sight. I want to lure him near the fire."

Lisa wasn't sure what Taylor had in mind, and she wasn't positive she could move Rick because he was easily 210 pounds. She backed away, keeping an eye on the gross figure coming for them then peeking over her shoulder to make sure she didn't stumble over her boyfriend. She noticed he was sitting up, supporting himself with one hand and grasping his damaged leg with the other.

"Rick, can you make your way to that tree behind you?"

Rick looked around, saw the tree and looked back to see the events unfolding in front of him. He half lifted his body and scooted to the tree. His injured leg was sending his brain all sorts of nasty signals that he was indeed seriously screwed, but his adrenaline was helping him to overcome that for the time being. He slammed into the tree, bruising his shoulder as the force of his body caromed off the bark, but it had him out of the path to the fire.

Taylor was taunting the zombie, for all the good she thought it would do, trying to buy Lisa and Rick some time. As she slowly made her way backward, she spit at the once-human thing and yelled, "Thought I was an all-you-can-eat buffet? Saw something fresh and tasty and wanted to take a bite. Only one guy gets to eat me, fucker, and it sure as fuck ain't you. You don't even have a tongue, you sick fuck."

Rick was pulling his Bowie knife from its sheath. He had never really used it but thought it would make him look cool and outdoorsy so he had brought it along. He didn't recall picking it up, but the old blade he had found earlier in the day had fallen free and laid on the pier. As he flashed the Bowie, he was trying to look around Lisa, who was a couple of yards in front of him and hunched in front of him in a protective stance. He could just see Taylor from between Lisa's bowed legs. Lisa had found a tree branch almost as long as she was tall and grasped it tightly in her hands.

"Damn, Taylor's got a mouth on her," he said.

Lisa didn't turn but she acknowledged him, replying, "You should hear her when she's pissed off. She'd make any sailor turn red from embarrassment."

Taylor was still calling the walking corpse every name in the book and a few that would need to be added to the lexicon at a later date. She had backed around to one side of the fire, the moaning creature following her while vocalizing the occasional snarl.

She could see the branch clutched in Lisa's hands from her periphery. As Taylor taunted the zombie she threw in a word or two here and there telling Lisa to come around from behind and plant the bastard's head into the forest. Lisa checked behind her and saw Rick sitting up against the tree, his Bowie reflecting the flicker of flames. She skirted around the fire in an attempt to fully get behind the zombie, circling around in partial darkness.

Lisa's accidentally kicked small pebbles along the path, the skittering noise attracting the zombie's attention. It paused in its advance towards Taylor. Taylor could see that Lisa wasn't close enough yet to get a good shot at the zombie. She took a chance and jumped forward with a front snap kick, her hiking boot smacking the zombie's remaining hand. The desiccated member flew up into the air, flipping wildly. The zombie turned to stare at its two stumps. The desiccated hand twirled between his two arms, crashing at his feet and breaking in two. The zombie's jaws dropped fully open as it tilted its head back on the few strands of muscle keeping it attached to its neck. The furious howl was cut short as the dead branch connected with his skull, spinning it off into the fire. The remaining flesh melted off the bone and a nasty, green vapor floated from the fire.

"Ooohh, gross," Lisa said, lowering the branch and looking away from the horror.

"Way to give him head, babe."

Taylor had her back to Rick as he made his vulgar comment. She just shook her head and rolled her eyes as she said to herself, "Fuck, he's back."

Lisa heard her and giggled, then screamed. She yelled out Rick's name and pointed behind him.

Rick whipped his head around and brought his knife up in front of his face, his right forearm blocking his throat. He had seen something similar in a couple of movies to prevent a garrote from being slipped around the neck and strangling the intended victim. Not that he could, or would, imagine why an undead monster would go for a piano wire or rope versus their teeth and claws. He hadn't seen what attack he was blocking against. Rick was the type to react first and ask questions later unless he was following a pattern laid out in practice or on the field.

The zombie sneaking up behind him had failed to study the playbook, coming in on Rick's left side and getting the best of him. A bony claw clutched Rick's chest. Despite most of the meat missing from the limb, the undead beast was strong, hauling Rick off his feet. The Bowie knife sliced across the rotting, upper arm. He felt the grip loosen, but it had not relented. Rick was up on his toes, his pulse racing with the additional pain the zombie was applying to his chest with infested fingertips rammed deep beneath his ribs. He drew back and let loose with a kick with his good leg, not sure whether a zombie had balls or not, but if they did he figured they were beyond blue and possibly purple and black. He bellowed in the rotting face, spit flying across the gangrene features, just like he did to Tech's quarterback last year in the final play when he sacked his opponent on the six-yard line. Rick's tackle won his team the championship. Now he followed his own mighty roar up by shoving the sharp blade deep within the zombie's chest, driving the pig sticker to the hilt then twisting it more than 90 degrees with both of his strong hands gripping the wood and steel handle with all his might.

Another howl erupted into the night, but it wasn't from the undead dropping Rick on his bad leg as it crumpled to its knees. It tried its strength against the football player in a battle to remove the blade.

The howl came from another zombie, or at least the upper half of it, grasping Lisa's boot about the ankle and yanking her foot from under her, tumbling her to the ground. It had crawled up on her from behind, hidden within the darkness.

Lisa screamed, dropping the dead branch and bracing herself for the ground, which was rapidly approaching her face. She caught most of her weight, but the fall knocked the breath from her as she bounced against the hard soil. She wanted to save Rick but she had to save herself first. She kicked with all her might, but the demi-zombie was making its way up her body, using her clothing to pull itself upwards. Her kick did little more than shake the creature.

Taylor rushed to her friend's aid, getting behind the remains of what looked like a woman who had possibly been in a car accident or maybe just half eaten by other undead. Taylor pulled the long, straggly hair, but the clump of strands just popped loose from the skull, the sucking sound of the separating flesh from bone like a large straw slurping mushy worms.

Lisa was still trying to crawl her way to the fire as Taylor grabbed at the partial monster's shoulders, attempting to dislodge the assailant. Lisa rolled to her side and Taylor saw her chance. She reached for the branch Lisa had dropped, swinging it around in one smooth move. She jammed it between the decomposed body and Lisa's back. The tight grip the bony claws had dug into Lisa's jacket shredded the denim, but it and the flannel shirt she wore protected her from the dirty nails directly piercing her skin.

"I've got the branch wedge between. Pull away."

Lisa did as Taylor ordered, pulling herself along the ground and prying the dead body off. Taylor swept the corpse as if she were playing field hockey, tumbling it into the fire. More green vapor floated into the night sky amidst sparks crackling and flying into the air as Taylor stumbled with the exertion, tripping over the tip of a burning log. She dived forward and to one side, just rolling clear of the fire. She heard a crunch as she landed.

"Oh shit," Taylor said, rolling on the ground and clutching her right elbow.

Lisa was still on the ground, trying to catch her breath. She could just see through the dancing flames that Rick was hacking away at his opponent, the head already sitting to the side as Rick let his aggression go on the mutilated body.

"Rick, are you okay?" she asked.

"Just fucking him up, baby doll."

She craned her neck to see Taylor still down, curled up in a fetal position. She dragged her own body over to her friend.

"Taylor? Are you okay?"

Taylor unballed her body and turned to Lisa. She looked different in the firelight and without her glasses, which were shattered and crushed somewhere beneath her.

"I can't see and I may have dislocated my elbow."

"You saved my life," Lisa said, her hand extended to help pull Taylor up to a sitting position. "I owe you."

"Well, you can skip singing loud enough to wake the dead. I mean, what the fuck? Goddamn zombies creeping around. I've had all this shit I care for. I'll never watch *The Walking Dead* again."

Lisa laughed, which got Taylor to forget her own anger for a moment and laugh along with her.

"So what's your walking, talking tree doing over there? A roid rage moment?"

Lisa saw Rick was physically tearing the zombie to pieces, dismembering it as he grumbled and growled.

"I guess so. He's not leaving much evidence of the body, although the bloodbath is pretty obvious. "I don't know if this is like the movies and books, but did you get scratched or bitten?"

Taylor shook her head. "No, just bruised. You?"

"I'm not sure. My back hurts like hell."

"Turn around and take off your jacket."

Lisa turned, her back facing the fire, pulling the scrapped jacket in front of her and looking at it with dismay. Her blouse was white, but Taylor was unable to tell if it had blood on it or not without her glasses.

"Shit, I can't see much. I'm blind as a cave newt. Hey,

jockstrap, quit fucking around over there and come check on your girlfriend."

Rick didn't respond.

"Rick!" Taylor yelled, pissed at being ignored. "Limp your lame ass over here and see if Lisa has any infected scratches or bite marks."

Rick grunted and snorted. His head twisted in an odd angle then shot back with the rest of him slamming into the dirt in a fit of convulsions, busting the tourniquet free. He rolled and thrashed about, covered in blood and grime across the blue and white star of his Cowboys shirt. His body contorted, flailing into the flaming logs, singing his hair and side of his face.

"Oh, shit!" Lisa blurted out. "He's turning."

Taylor was beginning to stand, pulling Lisa up with her. "I guess that answers whether you're infected or not. You probably would've started turning."

"No, not Rick," Lisa cried.

"Shut up and run. And just in case, you stay in front."

"Why me?"

"First of all, I can't see and I need you to lead. Second, if you turn, at least I won't have you sneaking up behind me."

A primal scream erupted from Rick. He was beginning to rise, his body color now ashen gray where it wasn't burnt to a crisp or mixed with swaths of blood and deep purple bruises.

"Go!"

"I don't know if I can," Lisa yelled back. "I don't know where I'm going."

"Anywhere but here," Taylor screamed, shoving her friend forward with her injured right arm without trying to knock her back down. She clutched Lisa's belt with her left hand.

Lisa headed for the front of The Spinning Jug, afraid to go behind it in the darkness where Taylor encountered the first zombie. She could barely make out that the door was ajar.

"The door's open. We can get in."

"No," Taylor said. "We'll be trapped." She thought for a second and added, "Do we have a moment before Rick limps his way to us?" She assumed that his already injured leg and, she couldn't believe she was thinking this possible, his devolution would make him slower than the other zombies.

Lisa glanced back and said, "Yeah, maybe four or five seconds. Why?"

"See if there's a way to lock that door or close it off for a while."

Lisa made her way to the door, being cautious in case something jumped out at her. Taylor was still tagging along behind her, feeling a bit like a train caboose.

"The door seems solid. There's some lumber here that could be lodged beneath it. It might hold for a bit."

Taylor smiled. "Lead us a good distance from the zombie, but not too far. We want him to be able to track us."

"Are you crazy?"

"I have a plan. Trust me, Lisa."

Lisa began moving towards the River Run Log Flume. She weaved her way through the wooden trusses raising the slide up three stories high. The women hid behind one of the large beams, taking a chance to catch their breath and assess the situation.

"Is he still coming after us?"

"Yeah, you know he's not going to quit."

Taylor rubbed her sore and swollen elbow while she thought. "Can you hide me a little deeper in the shadows of this ride then run to your left a good distance without him seeing you?"

Lisa was worried, not liking the sounds of this plan, but she answered, "Yeah, but should we really separate?"

"Here's my idea. You run down a ways then come back out where he can see you. Once you have his attention and he changes course to go after you, dip back into the shadows and run back to me. Then we'll take off for the barrel ride again."

"Are you sure you didn't hit your head?"

Taylor huffed in exasperation. "Trust me, we just need to buy some time before he comes back over to the barrel."

"What if there are more of those things out there?" Lisa asked, wishing she had taken a piss before all this had started.

"Then just run back to me fast and don't get caught."

"What about you? You can't see them coming if there's another one out there."

"I'll yell for help. You just get to the other end as fast as you can and get him misdirected. Now quit stalling and haul that skinny ass between the big phallic woodies."

Lisa started to leave. She took a moment to turn and give Taylor a hug. "Be safe."

"You, too. Remember, you owe me so you've got to come back."

They both smiled, then Lisa turned and began her run, dodging in and out of the beams, not wanting to run a straight line in case something was up ahead and waiting. She wanted to make herself a difficult target.

She approached near the entrance to the ride without incident. She paused behind the operator's shack to make certain nothing was hiding in there. She reached in and pushed buttons and adjusted some knobs, doubting if anything had power or would work. As she suspected, there was no power but she had hoped to get lucky and cause a distraction for anything in the park while giving the duo time to run away.

"Damn," she said. "Here goes nothing."

She stepped out in the open, waving her arms and shouting Rick's name, the pain of the movement causing her back to spasm. Her white blouse was somewhat visible in the darkness. Then again, zombies managed to make it around without half a brain, an eyeball missing and another falling out of their head. So how they found prey was beyond her.

The zombified Rick did hear her. He stopped and twisted his dying body around in a rigid manner. He sniffed the air like a wild beast and growled then started his slow lurch towards her.

She felt pity for him, her strong boyfriend now a walking sack of bones, dragging his injured leg behind him and clutching at what was left of his ribcage over his heart. Maybe there was a way she could help him, maybe even save him. She knew she couldn't kill him—or unkill him. That would be asking too much, even if it meant his soul could rest in peace.

He clawed the air and let out a horrendous noise.

"Maybe not," she said aloud.

She jumped up and down a few more seconds, yelling for him to follow her. She slowly backed her way into the shadows of the log ride. She made certain he was still traveling her direction before sinking further back. She felt something sharp snag her sleeve and the prickly pain of something slicing her shoulder.

"Oh, no," she cried. She turned to meet her fate only to discover that she had caught a splintered piece of wood from one of the creosote-coated beams. She sighed in relief as she pulled her sleeve free. She checked her immediate surroundings the best she could in the gloom and it seemed free of any movement. She rushed back to Taylor as quietly as she could, hoping nothing foul had befallen her friend.

Taylor heard Lisa's rushing footsteps and assumed that it wasn't anything dead making its way for her. She called out Lisa's name in a loud whisper, receiving a positive response.

Once Lisa was back at Taylor's side, she told her that Rick

was slowly heading off in the wrong direction. Then she asked, "How long do you think before Darrin gets back?"

Taylor had been worried about Darrin ever since the first attack, wondering if he had made it through. She tried to remain positive for Lisa, but more for her own sanity. "He should be getting to the Jeep any time now. Hopefully, he won't be much longer.

"Come on, let's sneak our way back to the barrel. Try to move quickly and quietly, but slow enough to keep an eye out for Rick and anything else."

They traveled in the midst of the log ride uprights as much as they could before having to exit the safety of the structure and cross the uneven and cracked pavement, bypassing a couple of souvenir shops and a Kentucky rifle shooting range: air guns aiming at squirrels, coons and rabbits instead of little ducks.

"All right, The Spinning Jug is just across the way. Now what?"

"There's a thick rope coiled up behind it where the first dead son of a bitch came after me. I'm hoping it's long enough and strong enough to hold your weight."

"My..."

"Yes, your weight. I've got a little more muscle and a little more ass than you do, so it'll be easier for me to pull you up than you pulling me."

"I was correct. You hit your head and fried your brain on that fire pit," Lisa determined.

"No I didn't. Trust me, if the rope is strong enough then we can trap Rick and if there aren't any more undead out there we can either try and get away or sit by the fire and wait for Darrin."

"And if it isn't strong enough..."

Taylor pressed her fingers against Lisa's lips, and almost up her nostrils. "Then I'll know beforehand when I test it."

"Fine, but I'm not thrilled with the idea," Lisa said. Taylor couldn't tell that Lisa was shooting her a dirty look, which was rare for Lisa.

"It beats running from your doubly-brain dead boyfriend all night."

"Hey, that's not nice."

Taylor heard the hurt in Lisa's voice. She didn't necessarily feel sorry for Rick, but she hated that her friend was upset. "I apologize. But I don't want to keep running all night if he's the last of these fucknuts we have to deal with. I'd rather have him locked away so we know where he's at."

"I know. It just really stinks because I liked him a lot. I know he was a bit dimwitted and chauvinistic, but he would've done anything to protect us—both of us."

"You're right. And he did. I promise not to say anything bad about the once-living version of him again. But the dead version of him is going down. Agreed?"

Lisa nodded her head in agreement. She led Taylor across to the sidewall of the barrel ride. Taylor took out her phone.

"Here, find the app for the spotlight, but keep it covered so it doesn't give us away to Rick."

She handed the phone to Lisa, who hovered over the device with her back to the main area of the park. She found the app and turned the light to the ground at the back of the ride.

"The rope is near the adjacent corner. Watch your step for loose boards with nails and for zombie's with bigger nails."

"Yeah, got it," Lisa said as she began to sneak off.

"Oh, and don't step where I peed."

Lisa was nervous. To cut the tension she replied, "Maybe your scent was like doe piss to attract a buck. Only you attracted zombies."

"There is nothing dead up my twat. Now get moving before I do the zombie's work for him," she half-joked.

Lisa made her way down to the back corner of the ride while Taylor felt her way to the front of the ride, shuffling her feet and carefully searching for the lumber Lisa had mentioned, hoping to not impale her hand or foot on a nail or broken piece of wood.

Lisa stuck the phone around the back wall on the brightest setting then poked her head around. At first she saw only wall and overgrown flora. At the end of the wall, she saw a conical pile stacked nearly two feet high, which she assumed was the rope.

She quickly made her way to the rope and shined the light inside of the hole to make certain no critters were waiting for her to stick her hand in. Seeing it was safe, she placed the phone on the ground, just inches from a small puddle, and shoved her hand down through the hole and simultaneously reached beneath the rope from the outside edge. She tried to lift it.

"Holy shit, this is heavy," she exclaimed in a harsh whisper.

She tugged on it again and managed to lift the coil, heaving it over one shoulder. She bent over to get the phone and threw herself off balance, the wall being the only thing that saved her from taking a dive into the puddle. She repositioned and bent down once again, this time with success. She shined the light for a brief second around the corner and saw it appeared clear of Rick. She turned it off and moved as quickly and quietly as she could along the wall until she got to the front. She could see the silhouette of Taylor moving around, shifting boards.

"Rawr," she said in a teasing whisper.

Taylor jumped and turned. "I will lock your ass in the Jug with him, I swear to God."

Lisa giggled.

"Got the rope?"

"Yeah. There's a staircase here beside me."

"Good, let's get up there and find something to tie the rope off. If we have time I'll try and put a few knots in the rope to make it easier to climb."

Lisa looked at the heavy rope. "It's not going to be easy to tie. This thing is thick. Sort of like Rick."

"Oh, so you can make jokes about his lack of intelligence and I can't?"

"I wasn't talking about that head," Lisa said with a smile that Taylor couldn't distinguish, but she could hear it in the way she said it.

"Seriously?"

"Oh yeah," Lisa replied.

"So that's where the blood supply went. No wonder you liked him."

Lisa just giggled some more.

"Come on, tramp. Let's get up the stairs."

Taylor stuck a hand out in front of her and let Lisa guide her. She let Lisa go up first so she could hold onto the handrail with her sore arm and placed her other hand at Lisa's back to help balance her with the rope. When they got to the top, Lisa explained what they had to work with, which was a rail that encircled the barrel from above and a six by six beam every five feet with a roof above the structure.

"Toss one end of the rope down in the barrel and let me know how much we have to work with up here."

Lisa did as told. She guessed, "Maybe three or four feet of rope."

Taylor thought for a moment. "Okay, not enough to wrap around two posts, but enough to put a knot every foot or so and I can tie it off to one post. I wish we had a pulley then I could pull you up a lot easier."

"Well I wish we had a flying carpet so we could just get out of here."

"You're getting awful sassy in your old age," Taylor said. She couldn't see Lisa sticking her tongue out at her. "Okay, pull the rope up while I tie this end off."

Five minutes later, Taylor had the rope the way she thought would work. She pulled on it and felt up and down the entire length, testing it for any weak spots. It was plenty frayed, covered with mildew. Individual, coarse strands poked into her palms, but overall she trusted it would hold.

Meanwhile, Lisa stayed hunkered down at the top of the staircase, keeping watch. She could see Rick wandering around, lost, confused and moaning once he discovered she was no longer where he last saw her. She saw no other movement in the park, so maybe he was the last one.

"You ready to go?"

Lisa looked back at Taylor. She wanted to say "no" but knew she had little choice.

"Get his attention and make sure he sees you enter the Jug. Once he gets close, you begin climbing the rope but keep calling out to him so he'll enter. Who knows, he might be smarter as a zombie…"

"You promised."

Taylor sighed, "Sorry. At any rate, he might sense it's a trap and refuse to enter unless he can hear you. Get high enough he can't grab you. I'm going to hide near the bottom of the stairs. Yell when he enters and I'll close him in and brace the door with the boards. Then I'll come back up to pull you over the rail if you haven't made it already."

"That's a lot of things to do for a half-blind girl and a fully scared one," Lisa said.

"I know, but you can do it. We can do it. Who knows," Taylor said as she tried to disguise the doubt in her voice, "maybe if we can get back to civilization we can tell the authorities and they can find a cure or some shit for him."

"Do you think so?" Lisa asked full of hope.

"At the very least they can make a cast of his big schlong and cast you a dildo before it rots and falls off."

"You are so gross."

"Go entice Rick the Dick so we can trap his undead ass." Taylor gave Lisa one more hug before she felt her way down the stairs and ducked beneath. She placed a couple of smaller boards up vertically to give her a bit more cover.

Lisa turned Taylor's phone back on, using the light to shine in Rick's direction. It wasn't bright enough to shine on Rick, who was nearly the distance of a football field from her, but between her yelling to him and waving the light, she was certain she could get his attention. She spent several minutes, calling out to him every fifteen seconds or so, knowing it was going to take him a long time to make it to her. After a few minutes, Rick was finally nearing the end zone—and so was the phone's battery. The light flashed erratically before the device beeped and died.

Lisa reached for her back pocket, rushing to pull out her own phone. She knew she had Rick's attention, but she wanted to make sure she could see her way in the Jug without tripping and could find the rope. She patted her pocket then frantically searched the ground.

Taylor couldn't tell what was going on. She assumed the phone had died when she could no longer see the light, but she had no idea what Lisa was doing. She could tell she was moving, and another blur in the distance was moaning, so Rick was coming. But she didn't know why Lisa wasn't making her way to the door. She didn't want to call out and give her position away or it could ruin the trap. She chose to do a whippoorwill call, a nocturnal bird that would hopefully get Lisa's attention without drawing too much attention from her zombie lover.

Lisa realized she no longer had her phone. It had been in her back pocket. She thought that maybe it was lost when the female half-zombie jumped her back. She heard the bird call, the first bird she had heard all day. She knew it must be Taylor.

"Shit, shit, shit," she cried out as she made her way back to the Jug. There was practically no light for her to follow. Even the glow of the fire was almost nonexistent, as the fire had been burning down while they had been battling the undead.

With the exception of the broken pavement, she knew she had a relatively clear path back to the front of the ride. She would have to watch her step once she approached the door so she wouldn't trip over boards or slam her face into the door. Her eyes were acclimating to the darkness, but with the cloud cover, it was nearly pitch black. Why they hadn't thought of taking a second to grab a flashlight from their packs angered her, but she knew they really hadn't had time.

She stumbled along, her hands in front of her, barely able to see the outline of the ride and the partially open door. She pulled it open, the creaking hinges erupting in the night like a crack of lightning. She heard a loud moan and looked behind her. She couldn't really see him, but the faster shuffling of his feet and the loud moans gave her reason to believe that zombified Rick seemed excited at hearing the sound—or maybe that he thought he could trap his lost love and have her for dinner.

With shaking hands and trembling lips, Lisa called out, "Come on, Rick. Come to Lisa. You can do it."

Another series of moans encouraged Lisa to hurriedly step over the half-foot high metal frame at the bottom of the doorway. She partly closed the squeaky door, hoping the sound of Rick having to pull it back open would be a clear enough signal that he was close since she could barely see him.

"Oh, man, I thought it was dark out there," Lisa said. The interior of the Jug blocked out even more light. She could see the slice of lesser darkness where the door was still partially open. She was trying to recall if she had seen anything from above when she looked down at the floor that might be a tripping hazard. She thrust her hands in front of her once more and made her way to the area where she believed the rope was hanging.

For the first couple of seconds, once she reached the rounded interior, she panicked. She couldn't find the rope and began to doubt she had chosen the correct direction. Her breathing became labored and she felt tears welling up in her eyes as the noisy hinges began to slowly creep open. A quick sweep to the left and her hands brushed against the rope. She let out a gasp of relief.

Looking over her shoulder, she could see the door was now hanging open much wider. The sinister shadow that was Rick seem to suck all the lighter darkness into his body like a black hole—a black hole that wanted to swallow Lisa up and shit her out of the asshole of the universe.

She grasped the rope with a renewed urgency, pulling her body upwards a slow inch at a time as she tried to get high enough to get her foot on the first knot.

If I survive this I swear I'm going to start working out, she thought, her thin, tanned arms barely containing enough strength to pull her slender body up the rope. She remembered the days in P.E. when the boys and more athletic girls would laugh at her because she hadn't been capable of climbing the rope. At that time she didn't care because she didn't want to be an Amazon and most of the boys found her to be one of the hottest girls in school. Now she was regretting being so vain.

She looked at the doorway and realized the obscured shaft of lighter darkness outlined no bulky figure, which meant that Rick was probably somewhere in the Jug with her and she had no clue where.

"Holy fuck! Taylor, I think he's here! I can't see him!"

The response was the door slamming closed, followed by the banging of boards as someone propped it closed. Hopefully, it was Taylor. Lisa's fear was growing by leaps and bounds as her adrenaline kicked into overdrive. She had found the first knot that was low enough to get a foot on and had her hands clutched tightly around another knot just above her head. She scrambled, the sound of her feet and knees banging against the interior wall and echoing around the circular chamber. The racket was answered by a nasty growl. She knew for certain that was near. She could almost taste the iron in the air; Rick's leg wound having fully bled out. His pants and shoe were saturated with his own blood.

In return, Rick could smell Lisa's fear, terror racing through her veins and her heart about to explode. The squishy juiciness of it excited him. He advanced, smearing a gory stain in his wake that went unseen in the coal-dark pit they meant to be his grave.

"Taylor, hurry and help me up," Lisa screamed, anguish and despair causing her voice to rise to a pitch that was meant for dogs—or possibly blood-thirsty coyotes—if such rabid beasts were roaming the area.

The pounding of footsteps hurrying up the outside staircase rattled and boomed like pealing thunder. Lisa was pulling herself up to the next knot, the exertion draining her energy. She could see the lip of the Jug and she figured she was only halfway there, which meant...

A strong hand grasped one of her hiking boots. She let out a bloodcurdling scream and was answered by a mutant roar from below her. She erratically kicked at the zombie with both feet, making contact but unable to break free.

She felt a warmth trickle across her buttcheek and down the inside of her thigh. The warmth traveled down her leg and into the captured boot. She didn't care. She kept screaming and kicking, but the extraneous movement was wearing on her. She could feel her arms trembling and knew she wouldn't be able to hold on for much longer.

She felt her body changing position. At first she thought Rick was pulling her down—imagining that his mouth was hyper-extended and he would just pull her down into his gaping maw where she'd disappear down his throat, piss-filled boot and all. But she realized that she was being slowly pulled upward, going up an inch or two then dropping back down about half the distance only for the process to be repeated. Looking up, she could see Taylor's silhouette from the waist up, hunched over and grunting with effort with the thick rope in her hands.

What Lisa couldn't discern was Taylor had the rope high enough now that she could wrap it once around her good arm to help heave her friend to safety. Her injured arm was threatening to break off. She hadn't thought of that when she suggested Lisa be the bait due to her size. She also had a leg shoved against the railing for support, preventing her from going over the side and landing at Rick's feet. She could hear the aged and weathered board protesting. She felt the center bowing, threatening to bust any moment and send them tumbling to their deaths.

She tugged, pulling Lisa up, but not as high or as fast as she had hoped. She couldn't see much of her friend and nothing of Rick. She wondered if the rope was hanging on something or if Rick had ahold. She yanked with all her strength, her arms and shoulders burning, the muscles nearly spent as the rope jerked to and fro, her elbow threatening to rip loose.

"Lisa, what's going on?"

"He's got my foot. I can't shake him loose."

Lisa raised her free leg as high as she could, letting loose her vitriol as she yelled, "Let me the fuck go, you goddamn bastard!"

This time as she kicked she let her hands slide a bit, the bristly fiber skinning her palms. She ignored the pain as her heel crushed the side of Rick's face. She could hear the solid impact and felt something give as his cheekbone was wedged up behind his eye socket.

His grip on her boot was released as the injured monster screamed in pain. Taylor could feel the difference and began pulling with renewed strength. Lisa was close enough Taylor could hear her friend's heavy breathing over her own.

The jubilation was brought to a quick end as the rope was pulled tight again as Rick grabbed it, trying to pull Lisa back down to him. He shook it back and forth, trying to dislodge her. Lisa was repeatedly slammed against the wall, banging her elbows and the back of her head and her sore back against the hard surface. She had her face tucked between her forearms to protect herself the best she could.

Taylor wasn't sure what to do. She knew she couldn't hold

the rope much longer and that Lisa would slip back down close enough to be grabbed. Then she had a thought.

"Hold tight," she yelled down to Lisa.

Taylor hopped up just enough to let her other foot slide forward, slamming both of her knees into the weakening two by four. She could feel Lisa drop a little but she didn't have much choice. She readjusted her grip on the rope with her left hand, which was the side the lifeline was wrapped around. She tenuously let her grip loosen with her right hand, ensuring herself she could hold the rope for a few seconds with the other. She jammed her right hand down into a deep pocket of her cargo pants, grasping a mixture of loose change. She yanked her hand free and drew it back all in one motion, her shoulder bunching up and cramping. She threw the change into the darkness of the Jug.

A dozen metallic clinks pinged against the far wall of the Jug, rebounding and falling to the metal, drop-away floor. The coins clanked, rolled and whirled to spinning stops. It had the effect Taylor was hoping for. She felt the taut line loosen. Rick had let go to investigate. She was sure that would've worked on him in his living, breathing form, but she wasn't sure if the brain-dead version would fall for the distraction.

She grasped the rope by both hands once more, one of the knots quickly moving close enough for her to reach over it and increase her grip. Four more pulls and she could see the top of Lisa's head cresting the rim. She pulled a little more until she felt Lisa's hand smack the lower board that her knees were braced against, the fingers curling over between Taylor's knees. Now it was much easier to pull Lisa up with her supporting part of her own weight on the board. Then she felt Lisa's other hand make contact with the board on the other side of her right knee.

"Do you have a good hold?" she excitedly asked.

Lisa was in tears as she cried, "Yes."

"Letting go of the rope," was all Taylor said as she simultaneously completed the action. She quickly leaned over the upper rail, the edge of the board cutting sharply below her ribs.

"Reach up and grab on."

Lisa let go of the board with one hand and flailed in the partial darkness, her hand and wrist smacking Taylor's twice before she managed to lock her small hand around Taylor's wrist. Then she let go with her left hand to grab the other wrist. She heard Taylor grunt as her full weight pulled Taylor hard against the wood.

Taylor grunted louder and yelled out as she was slammed down on the board. A loud pop could be heard. The rope was still wrapped around her left arm and Rick had returned.

Between gritted teeth she swore, "If you weren't already dead I would kill your fucking ass." Sweat dripped from her upper lip, landing on Lisa's forehead, which was getting closer as she had managed to get one foot over the edge. She let go with one hand and pushed herself up, finally letting go with both so she could squeeze beneath the lower rail and the landing.

Taylor scooted to the side as much as she could. Now that she had both hands free she yanked back on the rope that was biting and burning all the way down her arm. She knew her left elbow was going to be a giant bruise, if not broken. But Taylor was angry as hell. She pulled the rope enough to get her arms back over the rail then planted her feet against the narrow lip of the landing meant to keep shoes from errantly kicking a pebble or food off into the face of an unsuspecting rider. She braced herself and gathered enough slack to where she could feel the pressure of the rope loosen. She was too weak and injured to hold the rope with just her right hand as she tried to get free.

Lisa was just getting up to her hands and knees. She reached out and assisted, pulling on the rope just in front of Taylor's left hand.

"I've got it," Lisa said.

Taylor let go. Lisa was yanked sideways, slamming into the lower rail. If she had only seen darkness before, she could now see stars, the board solidly contacting her temple and across her ear.

Taylor was pulled forward as well, but she quickly got her arm out of the coil. The throbbing exploded down her shoulder. She thought the trapped blood was now trying to blast out of her fingertips as it began circulating once more.

"Owww! Fuck me! Let go, Lisa."

Lisa gladly did so.

"You all right?" Taylor asked.

Lisa felt the side of her head. "There's no blood, but it's gonna be a heckuva bruise."

"Can you stand?"

"I think so."

"Go over to the other side and get his attention."

"What are you going to do?"

Taylor grimaced. She had to use her arms to help push herself up, her legs shaky and her adrenaline reserve near empty. "I need him to let go of the rope so I can untie it. I don't want to risk him being able to climb out."

Lisa nodded her head then quickly regretted such movement as the stars and nausea returned. She gave herself a moment to regain her equilibrium before utilizing the rails to pull herself up. She winced, realizing that her ankle was probably sprained after what Rick had done. She leaned heavily on the rail and hopped her way 90 degrees around the deck.

The hopping footfall on the metal landing grabbed the zombie's attention. He watched her hobble back towards the direction of the door. His zombie brain was like a dog with two bones, hoping he could eat her and, in addition, she might open the door and let him escape. He let loose the rope and Taylor quickly went to work.

Rick reached up, clambering for his lost love while limping over to Lisa. She still couldn't see him but she could hear him moving about, getting nearer. The tip of her boot smacked something metallic. She reached down and found it was a lead pipe, almost the length of her arm and nearly as big around. It was very heavy. She looked over the side and called out.

"Oh, Rick, honey? Riiicckkk," she said in a sweet, enticing voice.

She heard a soft moan and footsteps that approached closer then stopped. Another gurgling growl rose up in the night air from a head thrown back and eyes staring up longingly at the beautiful girl covered in dirt, bruises, scrapes and sweat with her teeth clenched together. Beauty blindly dropped the lead pipe into the pitch black. She smiled as she heard the satisfying thunk of metal against flesh and bone, followed by the Beast dropping to the floor with a dying cry echoing off the round wall and spiraling up to the void.

THE TWINKIE TRAP

Gus heard Jessie's ear-piercing scream all the way across the former gift shop on Mud Island. He rolled out of his cot, his bare feet slapping down on the hard floor. He raced through a dimly lit room that once held Mississippi River, American Indian, Elvis and other Mississippi Delta music memorabilia. He stubbed his toe on a rotating wire magazine rack, almost knocking it over. As he hopped he grabbed his big toe, which was now throbbing. He could feel the yellowed toenail was dented in considerably and he sensed wetness along the cuticle. *Probably bleeding*, he thought.

In the few seconds it took for Gus to grab his smelly foot and try to determine if his toe was broken, the hilt of the skinning blade in the scabbard he wore at all times hung up in the metal wire. Gus was pulled off balance and then the rack spilled over, tripping Gus up as it plummeted with a loud crash, spilling pamphlets and brochures.

"Sonuvabitch," Gus grunted as he wrestled with the rack and kicked himself free. "Jessie? Jessie? What the hell's wrong? Where are you?"

As he finally got his left foot untangled, he saw a pair of well-worn steel-toed boots in front of his face. Looking up the shapely and tone bare-skinned legs that stopped where they met a very, very short pair of Daisy Duke cutoffs without a hem. The little frayed bits of white string hanging all around the bottom of the shorts stood out against her velvety black skin, dangling in front of his eyes. He wanted to pick at the strings, just to pull them loose and unravel them to see how much of the denim would disappear and reveal more skin.

Gus knew he shouldn't be thinking things like that. Jessie was his Aunt Margaret's daughter. He just couldn't help himself. There weren't many real humans left on the planet, most of them turning into dadgum zombies about four years back. Jessie was only 15 then. Now she was coming up on 19, just six years younger than Gus. He had a little bit of a beer gut and he hadn't shaved since he was probably 15, so his face was a bit of a scraggily brush pile. But he was still a thin guy with not much muscle to speak about. He'd been a lazy, pot smoking, hip-hop jamming brother who hung with his boys when he wasn't working. He liked the late night shift because business was slower and most of the people coming in to buy gas, Pop Tarts or papers were as buzzed as he was.

Jessie had managed to find razors right after the zombie apocalypse. She even found stuff to fix her hair on occasion. She was smart when it came to the early choices, letting most folks fight over food and beverages when all hell broke loose. She knew she'd be surviving with people doing that battle. So she stayed clear of most of the masses and got the essentials for herself and even extras, like toothbrushes and such, for Gus, Alton Lee and Big Dawg, Jr.

Alton Lee was Jessie's daddy. He was a tough man with leathery skin from his years working the cotton fields around the Memphis and West Memphis region. He didn't take shit from no man or zombie. Gus figured that Alton Lee had probably downed more of them dead fuckers than all the other survivors combined, and his uncle wasn't particular with what he used for a weapon or whom he used it on.

When the change first happened, half of the cotton plantation turned that day. Alton was operating the cotton picker when four of his co-workers, whom he'd known for 20 plus years, came scrambling after him through the cotton rows, faces all pale and jaws slackened with their blackened tongues hanging out and drool dripping down their overalls. He recognized Buddy Destri gnawing on someone's arm.

Turned out to be the limb of the plantation's Driver. Despite slavery being done and gone for 150 years, the terminology remained as did the fact that the Driver, Chester Townsend, was a white man whose job it was to oversee the fields, keep the workers busy and make certain things were being done properly so as to bring in a profit. He was a snotty bastard. He and Alton lee had come close to blows several times, but Townsend knew that if Alton Lee walked then the rest of the crew would follow behind him. The only reason Alton Lee never took a shot at Townsend is because he had a large family to raise, times were tough and he was getting too damn old to start job hunting and starting over for minimum wage.

Alton Lee didn't think long or hard on his current situation. If the three men and the woman were approaching him while eating body parts, then he wasn't going to wait and ask them questions.

"Buddy Destri," he yelled from the cab of the spindle style

picker, "I's glad that you et that waste of space Townsend, but ya'll ain't gonna eat me."

Alton Lee revved the engine as the zombies roared in defiance. The roar didn't last long as the picker, with its wide row of barbed spindles, belched black smoke and moved forward. The zombies were oblivious to their imminent demise as the spindles snagged and ripped at them, pulling them through the doffer with its quick weight loss plan and blowing bits of them into the basket—and across the field, splattering the white and green plant with red gore. It looked like Christmas had arrived in the fall and Santa got the shit blown out of him by one of them damn terrorists over a plantation.

Alton had to take out a few more zombies as he drove the picker 80 acres to the field gate, leaving a messy trail behind him. He figured he wasn't going to be getting paid no more, so he didn't give a shit if he cut across rows and left pieces of fucked up people in his wake.

He rescued a couple of others who weren't contaminated. No one knew for sure why some poor souls got the Z-virus, as it was called, and why some remained human, unless they got infected with a bite or nasty wound then odds were good they'd turn. Alton Lee lost his wife and nine of his children that day. He wasn't sure who all was infected and who was unfortunate enough to be turned by a zombie. All he knew is once he got home, still driving the harvester because his small truck had been flipped during the outbreak, he found some of his family dead in the yard, and some trying to attack anything alive. So he rolled over them and took the ramshackle house out with it.

Jessie, his oldest of 10 offspring, survived the harvester incident because she was in class taking a geometry exam. Her siblings hadn't been in school because they had either been too young, too sick or stayed home to help their mama. She came home to find her daddy kicked back in the cab of the picker, listening to B.B. King on the CD player as he drank a beer he found at a neighbor's abandoned house.

With him was a large man that was known as Big Dawg, Jr. No one seemed to know his real name but they knew him. He was a boiler maker at the plantation. He hitched a ride and rode shotgun while carrying an especially large wrench to take out any zombies approaching the harvester's flanks as Alton Lee drove down the highways, side streets and across devastated lawns filled with house items or body parts.

Being a boiler maker at the cotton plantation gave Big Dawg the skills to also build smaller boilers, like the one that was now set up behind the gift shop. He made some fine shine that could practically peel the paint off any surface and guaranteed to kill more bacteria than a can of Lysol. A Mason jar of Big Dawg's home brew would have anyone off in la-la land before long, forgetting all their cares and worries. It took a little more for Big Dawg to go under, so he generally kept a beautifully handcrafted sterling silver flask on hand. It was shaped like a hollow-body electric guitar and intricately carved.

Big Dawg also lived up to his name. He was a large man, standing 6' 2" and weighing in at a little over 300 pounds. He was very protective, probably stemming from his high school days playing defense. He was fast for a big man and any unfriendly person or non-person getting within range of whatever Big Dawg happened to be swinging at the time—lead pipe, wrench, two by four, his huge fists the size of softballs—normally ended up with their head splattered and their ribcage caved into their spine.

It was a good thing he and Alton Lee got along, because Alton Lee didn't know how to back down and a brawl with Big Dawg would've been ugly. Alton Lee wasn't small, but he wasn't as large as Big Dawg. But he could fight—and he fought to live, call it dirty fighting if you like. He figured that any fight he could walk away from was a good one, even if he resorted to some underhanded tactics. Not that zombies were exactly lining up and filing complaints when Alton Lee almost single-handedly rid the Island of the undead.

Jessie had suggested Mud Island because it only had a couple of roads to get to the mainland, sitting out in the Mississippi River. An amphitheater was the main draw back in the pre-apocalypse days. Bands would perform music and families would enjoy the Mud Island River Park or the museum. She figured that the island would limit access if they could guard or block off the roads, praying that the zombies wouldn't be able to cross the water without being swept downstream.

As they made preparations, *borrowing* survival items such as food, rope, flashlights and weapons from any abandoned house or neighborhood store that still had anything left, they found Gus, hiding behind a counter at the gas station where he worked the graveyard shift.

Gus wasn't a coward, but he also wasn't about to go out in the streets on his own during the outbreak. Before the trio found him, Gus had pulled the sawed off shotgun from under the counter for defense and snacked on beef jerky, Twinkies and RC Cola. He only came out from behind the counter to sneak off to the restroom to take a piss or if he heard someone rummaging around, looting. As long as they didn't fuck with him he didn't care what they stole at this point. He could see their reflection in the security mirror back behind the counter. Most of the intruders had been human. A couple of times zombies had wandered in, but none had ventured far enough into the store to force him to reveal his hiding place and blow them away.

When he first saw the trio come in the store, sweat poured down his forehead and dripped into his eyes. The one figure was large and carried a wrench and a pistol. Another was carrying a rifle, smoking a cigarette and looked like he meant business. The third, he could tell, was female, but in the mirror it was difficult to identify the people.

"Gus, is yo scrawny ass in here, boy?"

"Is that you, Uncle Alton?" Gus yelled from underneath the counter, still shaking with fear.

"Where you at, son? Get with it. We's traveling up the river bank and headed to the Island."

Gus came out of hiding, clutching the shotgun tight to his chest. He saw his uncle and cousin along with the huge man he didn't know. He lowered the weapon as Jessie came running around the corner and hugged him. More than his sawed-off was stiff, straight and ready to blow.

"Get whatever shit you need? Ain't much left on yo shelves, but we's leaving in two minutes," Alton Lee said. He and Big Dawg searched for anything of use.

"You okay, Jess?" Gus asked.

She was trying not to break down, but tears welled in the corners of her eyes and threatened to roll down her beautiful cheeks. "Mama's dead. So's the rest of 'em. Papa had to kill 'em cause they all turned into this shit going around."

She hugged Gus again, but this time he hugged her back with true sympathy. He liked his Aunt Margaret. She and his mother were the last two siblings from a family of seven. Their brothers, his uncles, had all died fighting in various deserts across the Middle East; all earning purple hearts that did the family no good except make them proud. It didn't bring back their husbands and fathers.

Now they were in another war, one of horror against undead

family and neighbors. Gus was trying not to shed tears of his own as Jessie's warm, salty drops landed on his shoulder and she boo-hooed quietly.

He saw Alton Lee approach and place his hand on Jessie's shoulder, probably one of the only times Gus had ever seen his uncle being loving. Not that he didn't love his family, but he didn't coddle them. He had to work hard to make a living and provide for them. When he got home he expected they all had done their chores and he didn't put up with no lip or shit. He'd pull his belt off in one quick motion and leave welts on the backside of anyone fucking up or not pulling their weight. Seeing him being gentle with Jessie was a rarity.

Jessie raised her head and released Gus as her papa said, "Time to go, little girl. Yo idea for the Island is good. We's still got a long and treacherous walk ahead of us and we don't know what we's gonna find when we's get there."

Jessie grabbed the razors and other toiletry essentials she figured they'd need. Gus grabbed a couple of large trash bags and stuffed them full of junk food and canned goods like Vienna Sausages and Spam that was locked away in the stock room and hadn't been looted yet. He grabbed the half-full box of .12 gauge shells from the safe. He left the cash. It was worthless green paper.

Leaving from south Memphis, they cautiously made their way as fast as they could. At times they would see a band of undead loping about. They chose to hide instead of fight, not risking whom they had left and not wanting to take the time to battle and draw attention to possibly more zombies. Off in the distance they occasionally saw a lone human or a couple running, ducking down, hiding the same as they were.

They eventually traveled past the Rivergate Drive area where the Wonder Bread Distribution Center was located. It was locked up tight that dreadful night four years ago when the four survivors passed by; carrying about all they could handle at the time. Gus kept the warehouse in mind for future reference, hoping there would still be food inside.

By morning, as the sun broke over the horizon of a disaster area, they made their way to the crossing over Wolf River harbor, a part of the Mississippi, and saw that most of the damage had already been done. There were abandoned cars in various states of destruction along with various bits and pieces of people and zombies scattered all over. It was disgusting, reeked of death and was desolate. They didn't see another soul all the way across, just more death, along the steps to the museum and across the cobblestone. The monorail was on fire and bodies were strewn everywhere. Most of the museum was destroyed, including all the ancient artifacts and rare, historical pieces.

Surprisingly enough, the gift center had sustained little damage. Most people had run out of there the minute the change happened. The store manager shut down the entrance, locked it and blocked it off. She later escaped out the back door, leaving it unlocked in case she had to make a hasty retreat back to safety.

Big Dawg discovered the unlocked door. He called to the others as he went in, ready to kill anything that moved. It eventually became their home. They set up discreet areas for sleeping. They left most of the displays up so they could hide or, if someone else came around, would think it was nothing more than an abandoned shop. With the exception of some snacks and drinks, maybe the T-shirts, there wasn't much in a gift shop of survival value for looters to bother.

After a long day's rest, they made their way back across the river and over to the Pyramid, once a bustling place for events now turned into a huge ass Bass Pro Shop. Most of the weapons, lanterns, clothing and such had been taken already. Even the kayaks and canoes were missing, taken by people trying to get away and probably hoping that the state of affairs would be better downriver. There were sleeping bags left and enough cots for three of them. Big Dawg slept on the floor because there wasn't a cot around going to hold him. As if everything was right in the world, a few fish swam lazily around in the vast tank display. The group caught the fish for meals. They knew no one was going to come around and care for or feed the fish. They figured there was no sense in either of them suffering death by starvation.

Within a week they had the gift shop set up pretty much the way it still stood when Jessie began screaming her head off. Gus looked up into her brown eyes.

"You all right, girl?"

"No. I went to get some Twinkies and the last box, the very last box, had a hole in the side and mouse turds all around. Nasty little mice ate all our goddamn Twinkies." She huffed, her bountiful chest rising and lowering just inches above Gus's head. He felt his pecker shift into overdrive, threatening to burst out of his pants.

"What the hell's goin' on? Zombies trying to get in," Alton Lee yelled as he burst into the room, rushing way from the back of the shop. "I's in the bathroom trying to do my bizness and you'se out here makin' all kinds of racket. And why you on the fuckin' floor? Don't you know how to walk, boy?"

Gus's hard on quickly went away. Alton Lee was standing right above him and Gus had quickly taken his eyes off his cousin's breasts. He managed to stand up and dust himself off.

"I was racing through the dark to find out what Jess was screaming about. I thought something was getting her."

Alton Lee looked at them both, expectantly. "Well?" He waited a second and neither answered him. "What the fuck is goin' on? What you screamin' yo fool head off about, girl?"

Jessie repeated the events. She thought her papa would be pissed about her freaking out over a mouse. Not even a mouse, but the fact mice had gotten into their food stores, which were dangerously low. She awaited his berating.

"Motherfucka. Goddamn motherfucka." Alton Lee said in a harsh voice, his hands on his hips and his head shaking. "We's almost outta food as it is and fuckin' mice. All the dead people in the world and fuckin' mice and cockroaches gotta survive. They's worse than them smelly-ass zombies."

"Yes, papa," Jessie said, relieved that she wasn't going to be yelled at.

Gus's eyes lit up. He smiled and said, "Hey, last time we went out searching, me and Dawg noticed that the Wonder Bread place was still locked up. There was a hole in the chain-link fence. Why don't we try there and see if anything's left?"

Jessie wrinkled her nose. "That stuff is probably moldy or stale, assuming there's anything left."

"Nah," Gus replied. "Twinkies will last more than 50 years on the shelf."

"You know that's an urban legend, don't you? I think when they got bought out and Twinkies were put on the shelves once again, the Canadians managed to make Twinkies last for 45 days or so."

Alton Lee was rubbing his chin and thinking hard, weighing the risk against the possibility that their quest for Twinkies might be a lost cause. Finally, he said, "I say we's give it a shot. We'll go at nightfall. Big Dawg should be back by then."

"Yeah, where he be?" Gus asked. "I thought for sure he'd come hauling ass when Jess screamed."

"He's out burning the latest pile of them dead fuckers," Alton

Lee answered. "He carted a shitload of 'em over to the pile at the amphitheater. They's gettin' worse instead of better about coming across that bridge. I think we may have to blow those bridges up and use the paddle boats to get back and forth to the city."

Jessie knew they had no gunpowder or explosives. She asked, "Do we have enough moonshine to do that, papa?"

Alton Lee smiled, a grin that was broad and wide. There was a twinkle in his eyes. "We's may be low on drinkin' stock fo' a bit, but we's got enough to blow both bridges and still has a jug fo' a victory party afterwards. Check yo shit and get ready. We's goin' out tonight."

Between the lengthy distance of the walk back towards south Memphis and having to hide now and again from undead lumbering around, the trip back across Nonconnah Creek to the warehouse took them until nearly midnight to travel.

"There didn't use to be a fence around this place," Big Dawg said.

"They probably put it up to prevent vandalism and squatters," Jessie offered.

"Yeah, but there's still a couple of links cut so we can fold it back. Even Big Dawg can squeeze through," said Gus.

"Shit, it's gonna be a tight squeeze is what that's gonna be," said Big Dawg.

Alton Lee grabbed the loose wire and pulled back as far as he could. "Then you go through first, Big Dawg. I'll hold it fo' ya. Get yo scrawny ass over here, Gus."

Gus grabbed hold and tugged on the fence next to his uncle. Big Dawg ducked down and tossed his trusty wrench and pipe to the other side. He began forcing his way through the opening as Jessie kept watch. Fortunately, it was a pretty clear night. The moon was out, so she could see decently without having to use a flashlight and possibly attract more attention.

It took some effort, but Big Dawg made it through, only snagging his blood-stained Tennessee Titans shirt in a couple of places. He grabbed his tools/weapons and stood back up, taking stock of the situation to make sure they weren't going to be trapped in the parking lot by some wandering creatures that had somehow managed to get in. He saw nothing dangerous so he motioned for the others to come through.

Gus went next, followed by Jessie. Alton Lee made his way through and pulled the wire back flush, hoping no one passing by would notice it had been tampered with.

"All right, ya'll," Alton Lee whispered, "Eyes open and mouths shut. I don't care if it's livin' or dead, you hit to kill. Someone alive in here goin' to be awfully protective of they's shit. Odds are they's gonna try to kill ya if they find ya."

Gus and Jessie both silently gulped. They had killed zombies, and that had taken some getting used to. Killing a real human wasn't something they had expected. Big Dawg, on the other hand, skillfully tossed the pipe and wrench up in the air and grasped them with a new, firmer grip. He was ready to bust skulls.

"I bet I could send a zombie clean over the creek and hit one of the fuel tanks at the Valero refinery across the way."

Gus looked at Big Dawg and nodded his head in agreement. He was tempted to place a bet on it but he caught his uncle's glare and decided to keep his mouth shut.

They eased forward, trying to make as little noise as possible, spread out just enough they could swing weapons or bring up the barrel of a gun without poking one of their own. Granted, the ammunition had run out over a year ago, but the weapons were still imposing to the few living they caught snooping around. The weapons were solid and heavy enough to club a zombie with if need be.

Ahead of them were 11 bay doors to the concrete and tin building. A single tractor-trailer sat in bay nine, the once white Freightliner tagged with graffiti, the windshield busted and the tires flattened. The bay door was shut tight like all the others. Big Dawg, being as tall as he was, tested each of them.

"There's the Shipping door down by number one," Jessie said, pointing at a standard-sized door at the top of some steps. The steps ran along a wall that probably led to the offices or break room in the warehouse.

Big Dawg ascended the steps, taking up the entire landing. He tried the door but it was locked. The door's glass window wasn't large, maybe a foot square and eye level. Big Dawg shoved the pipe through the glass and wire security mesh on the flipside. He cleared the jagged edges then reached through. His arm wasn't long enough to reach the lock. He turned and pointed to Gus, motioning for him to get up there.

Gus timidly made his way up, searching for a place to stand without being squashed or knocked off. Big Dawg didn't even tell him what he was going to do. He just picked Gus up by the back of his shirt and his jeans, lifting him even with the window and crushing him up against the door.

"Stick your arm in there and turn that lock."

Gus pushed himself back from the door a bit so he could put his arm where his face currently was pressed. He threaded his arm through the opening and reached as far as he could. He felt around, his long fingers sliding over the lock a couple of times before he was able to grab the metal and twist the knob. He didn't have time to brag on his own achievement before he was being pulled back and lowered. Big Dawg let him loose while he was still in a horizontal position and four feet above the concrete. He dropped, his reflexes fast enough to keep him from landing on his face but not fast enough to fully get his feet beneath him. He landed in a contorted crouch, bruising a knee and skinning a palm.

"Fuck, Dawg, be a little gentler," Gus said.

Big Dawg turned, which consisted of his upper body starting to move then his feet having to make several steps to complete the process. He stared down at Gus, his eyes wide and his jaws locked tight.

"Please," Gus said, cowering back. "I meant be a little gentler next time, please."

Gus grunted and turned back to the door. He stepped down off the platform to give the door enough berth to bypass his large frame. He pulled the door open. A wave of musty, stagnant air hit him in the face.

"Damn, that smell's like dried up 90-year-old pussy."

Gus couldn't help but laugh, but he tried to keep the volume to a minimum. He looked up at Big Dawg who was still waving the stank away from his face. "You had a lot of experience with dusty old pussy there, Dawg?"

Dawg's bent over and his arm shot out to clutch the top of Gus's Bob Marley shirt. He snatched him up, leaving the scrawny man's feet dangling a foot above the pavement.

"Nigga, I will shove the rest of your black ass through that fucking window and use that scraggily, long-ass beard as a mop through the entire warehouse."

Gus's body didn't know what the fuck to do. His feet were desperately trying to reach the ground while his arms wrapped around the huge forearm of the man holding his life in his hands. He was attempting to pull his body higher and relieve the uncomfortable cinching of his shirt cutting into his underarm on one side and into his Adam's apple. The only thing his body had done right was quit laughing.

"Just jo...jok...joking," he managed, the words choking out.

"Big Dawg, let the little fool live. He be the only family I's got left besides Jessie. I's always thought he's a crack baby, but he's got his uses now and again."

Big Dawg dropped Gus once more. At least this time Gus was vertical, so he landed on his feet but still ended up in a crouch, trying to catch his breath and rubbing his body where the skin had been turned raw from his shirt.

Jessie helped him up as Big Dawg went through the doorway. His enormous hand reached for a light switch, just hoping, but nothing happened just like he figured. There were makeshift skylights that barely gave any luminance to the large space. In reality, it was just pieces of the warehouse roof missing and allowing the moonlight to peek through. Maybe it was done by vandals or zombies, but it was Memphis, so it could've easily have been a twister flying over. Tornadoes did funny shit, sometimes moving a home four inches off its foundation and not harming the house beyond that, only to leave nothing of the house next door except pieces the size of toothpicks and burst pipes spilling out water or gas.

He walked on through, swinging the wrench and pipe with medium force in case something stepped up to him that could see or sense him before his own eyes had time to adjust. He stepped forward another couple of strides then let the others know it seemed safe.

Alton Lee entered, a thick length of heavy chain in one hand and a flashlight in the other. He cut the darkness with the thin beam, wishing he had one of those fancy LED lights like the military used. The old flashlight he carried was almost dead and the light barely did more than light up an area about five feet in front of them.

"You kids get on in here before sumpin' out there eats ya."

Gus and Jessie made their way up the stairs and inside. Gus was still in pain but he played it up a little more than was necessary, letting Jessie place her hands on his butt and lower back to help get him up the steps. Then he slightly leaned on her once they were through the doorway, letting her support some of his weight. She couldn't see the sly grin on his face in the darkness, but Alton Lee had swung the light around and saw the two of them against each other. He didn't even see his nephew's face, just his torso.

"Boy, ya better learn to walk on yo own two chicken legs befo' I's break 'em fo' ya real good. You catchin' my drift?"

Gus quickly stood straight and stepped away from Jessie. "Yes, sir."

"Now get yo lights out and let's search. Jessie, you comin' with me. Gus, youse goin' with Big Dawg. I'd suggest you don't say nuttin' unless'n you gotta."

Gus turned on his flashlight and moved in front of Big Dawg, leading the way to the other end of the warehouse just a few feet parallel from the bay doors. Alton Lee and Jessie started out at an angle, also heading the to the far end of the warehouse, but closer to the back wall. Between their two lights they could see a little more than Gus since Big Dawg had both of his hands occupied with weapons. They all moved quietly, stepping lightly, more to listen for something coming at them than to prevent something from knowing they were present, as if their lights wasn't enough of a signal.

Because Alton Lee's light was weak, he walked closer to the wall, the beam bouncing back and spreading like oil in water as he searched. Jessie was just close enough that her light reached her dad when she turned it his direction. It reached to the middle of the warehouse when she turned away from him, but so far she had only seen more darkness. The warehouse was seemingly empty and there was nothing for the light to reflect off. But it was Jessie who found something.

"Papa, lookie here," she said excitedly in a loud whisper.

Alton Lee turned and saw something black and shiny, like Visqueen hanging like a curtain.

"Baby, shine yo light on up and see how high that damn thing goes."

Jessie did as her father ordered, the beam shining up and up. The light disappeared into the void, the warehouse higher and darker than her meager light could master.

"Damn, they's hidin' sumpin' behind that." Alton Lee moved up to the plastic sheeting, grabbing at the loose material, and trying to find an opening. He followed it down a ways, Jessie's light tracking him while his hands were busy searching. He found a corner where it ended on his side and met up with another wall of plastic. He brought his own light back up and pushed the material back with his chain-wrapped fist high enough to block his face if anything came at him. He poked his head through and blinked.

"Lawdy, lawdy, I's must be dreamin', Jessie. Look at dis."

Alton spread the plastic back further to allow her room to see. She damn near dropped her flashlight as she looked upon a pyramid of Twinkie cartons nearly two stories high and a bright halogen lamp hanging from the ceiling, illuminating the mother load. The Visqueen went all the way to the ceiling and draped all the way to the floor with some overflow, preventing a mysterious light from escaping the artificial room.

"Sumbitch," she mumbled.

"Youse got that shit right," her dad said with a short burst of laughter. "Big Dawg! Gus! Over here, ya'll."

"Where you at, unck?"

Alton Lee ignored his nephew and told Jessie, "Yo light be better than mine. Shine it over towards them thar doors."

Jessie pointed her beam at bay door seven. Moments later she could see Gus and Big Dawg rounding the corner at the other end, Gus's hand trailing along the sheet like a little kid with a stick along a picket fence.

"They got a tank hidden behind the curtain?" Gus asked, no longer attempting to stay quiet since his uncle had called out for them.

"Maybe better," Jessie said.

They pulled back the plastic and beheld the mountain of Twinkies in a halo of heavenly light.

"Well butter my ass and call me a flapjack," Big Dawg said in awe.

Everyone laughed at that rare burst of emotion from the big man.

"Big Dawg, " Alton Lee said, still laughing, "if'n they got a spatula as big as that goddamn stack of Twinkies, then I'll do just that and make Aunt Jemima proud."

Big Dawg began laughing as well.

"Y'all ever wonder why they call them what they do?" Gus asked.

"Whaddya mean?" Big Dawg asked.

"Well, you got Ding Dongs, which are cupcakes that are round, dark and filled with cream," Gus explained. "Then you got this phallic shaped, golden cake filled with cream, like the Man is trying to dis us once more. I may be dark like a cupcake but I'm shaped more like a Twinkie. Why don't they call the phallic one a Ding Dong?"

Jessie burst out laughing, covering her face as she snorted, embarrassing herself.

Gus squared up his shoulders and copped an attitude. "You think that's funny? What's so hilarious, woman?"

"I caught you whacking off behind the building one time. I'd have to agree. With that little thing," she said, pointing at his crotch, "you *are* more like a Twinkie. If the name fits..."

"Whooo, shit. She got you there, small fry," Big Dawg taunted.

Gus went to unzip his pants, trying to be all cool and shit. Jessie was still laughing, as were her dad and Big Dawg as Gus said, "I'll show you Twinkie!"

Alton Lee threw out his arm, catching Gus across the chest and stopping him from going any further. "Boy, you pull that trouser snake out and I's will whack it off with my knife and feed it to a goddamn zombie, I's swear on yo mama's grave. And I'll make you watch the shit happen."

"Fine," Gus said with disgust, pissed that the girl he wanted to impress was evidently unimpressed. His mind flicked back and forth between the current situation and trying to remember if he had known he was being watched at any time—and when was the last time he had stroked his meat behind the building. Was it after the time one morning when he happened to be walking past Jessie's sleeping area and caught a profile view of her putting on her bra and slipping her shirt down. He could swear he saw a bit of a nipple and felt he had no choice but to take care of business or walk around with blue balls all day.

"All righty, enough with teasing the handicapped. Let's go see about this stash," Alton Lee said, walking into the room.

Big Dawg followed, weapons at the ready.

Jessie gave a sly smile to Gus as she brushed past him. Her hand swept his crotch and she gave a quick squeeze to his balls but kept moving like nothing was going on.

Gus's mighty frown turned into a surprised smile that no one else saw. His soldier jumped to full attention, all four inches standing as erect as can be. He adjusted his pants before walking into the light. He decided to hold his flashlight in front of his pelvis with both hands like it was the cool, casual thing to do, just in case anyone was looking.

Jessie was to one side, and she was the only one glancing his direction, her eyes downward and a big smile on her face. The other two men were in front of her, silently debating about the pyramid. They couldn't see the slight bulge in Gus's jeans that

Jessie was witnessing. She turned away, trying not to laugh as he tried to readjust himself without seeming as he was trying to readjust himself—and failing miserably.

She had known for quite some time that her cousin was hot for her. She had even caught him trying to sneak peeks at her when she bathed or changed, but never let on that she knew. She just made certain that she was always concealed enough to keep him from getting more than a quarter's worth for the peepshow. She had no real sexual interest in him, but found teasing him was entertaining. She'd never even had sex, the outbreak happening while she was still a freshman in high school and she had been a good girl, not wanting to get knocked up like some of the girls she had in class. There were enough mouths to feed at her house—at least there were at one time—without her adding to the problem. She wanted to go to the University of Memphis and get her degree before getting married. She'd be the first one in her family and she wanted to make her folks proud. But the zombies shot that plan all to hell. She wasn't going to fuck her cousin or her papa. And even if it meant the end of mankind, she wasn't going to let Big Dawg ride her doggy style. That didn't mean she didn't have natural urges, but with her current choices, the answer was a big *fuck no, ain't no way in hell.*

When she looked back towards the Twinkie pile, she saw her dad moving up one side of the plastic and Big Dawg walking up the other side. They were both craning their necks to see if anything was poking their head from behind a sponge-filled box of banana cream, waiting to jump out. She slowly made her way towards the creamy center.

Gus followed her, the sawed-off from the convenience store in one hand and his turned-off light in the other. He quickly caught up with her and walked beside her, thinking maybe there was still a chance and maybe he needed to protect her fine ass. Gus wasn't too well read and was unaware of how history showed time and again that pussy made men stupid, dating all the way back to Adam and Eve up to the last president in office. Thanks to the outbreak of undead and the nearly-100% fatality of the communications industry, the media finally quit harassing the president about the leaked photos of a dominatrix pegging him. He claimed it was someone who coincidentally looked like him, despite the fact the carpet was obviously the same one in the oval office.

Now the media was dead. Rumor had it, so was the president. But with zombies trying to beat down everyone's door, no one really gave a fuck about either. They were more pissed about there being no more Starbucks on every other corner. Battling zombies would surely be easier with a CappaCrappaLacta-Free No-Fat Bean Whiz with extra Whipped Cream and Sprinkles. Maybe the mouse turds could pass for the sprinkles. That would be a start to rejuvenate the industry. Surely it couldn't taste any worse.

He wondered why zombies preferred people over, say, beef? Wasn't that meat, too? If zombies could just chill the fuck out and lurch their way up to the drive-thru window at Mickey Dees, order a couple of raw quarter-pounders, hold the rabbit food, maybe they could coexist with the humans and all would be righteous.

"Something's not right," Jessie said, snapping Gus out of his reverie.

"Why's that?"

"Why hide this stack only to throw a spotlight on it? If someone was hiding it for themselves, why put a light on it. If they aren't hiding it, why place the curtains around it? And why does this area have electricity and the rest of the place is without? Makes no sense unless it's meant to be a trap."

Gus didn't like the sound of that, so he gulped as quietly as he could. He thought for a second then said, "Maybe it was a trap four years ago. Now, whoever set it is dead. Like *dead* dead and not some undead fuck staggering around waiting to kill us."

"Maybe," Jessie replied.

The pyramid burst six stacks up in front of Jessie and Gus. It also burst in front of Big Dawg and in front of Alton Lee.

"Holy fuck! What da hell be happenin' now?" Alton Lee yelled, letting his chain uncoil from his fist, dropping nearly to the smooth concrete. He began swinging the linked metal, letting it gain momentum as the first zombie barreled forth from the tumbling pyramid, boxes cascading and bouncing, denting the corners and exploding open. The glue sealing the boxes shut was old and had sat in the warehouse for four years with no climate control, going from the icy cold of winter to the sultry heat of a Memphis summer with the humidity of the Mighty Mississip' pouring in.

Alton Lee's chain swung down dead center on the head of a zombie wearing a blue jumper and a hardhat. He had a name badge that Alton Lee wasn't taking time to read, but if he had to guess, the man worked in the warehouse at one time. The hard hat cracked wide open when a loud metallic *thunk* smashing plastic connected, but it saved his undead ass for the moment.

Almost simultaneously, two more zombies, one possibly a truck driver and the other was a man in a business suit. They let out animalistic yowls and made to attack Big Dawg. If the Visqueen hadn't been in the way, the resounding wallop he gave the suit's noggin had stood a good chance of at least hitting the creek, if not making it all the way to a flammable content storage tank on the other side.

The truck driver was more of a battle. He was nearly as massive as Big Dawg, even in his decimated zombie form. He had to have been at least a hundred pounds heavier when he was alive. He was probably in better physical condition now than he was when he was driving big rigs.

Big Dawg swung the pipe with mighty force. The driver was able to get an arm up. The crack of bone and cartilage echoed between the hard surface of the floor and the tin ceiling. The now-useless arm swung at an obscene angle from the elbow, but the driver still had both arms raised, trying to reach Big Dawg's throat. Big Dawg brought the wrench in from below, a formidable uppercut to the zombie's nuts, driving them up into his abdomen and forcing a desiccated organ to flop out of a gaping wound in the driver's belly. That slowed the zombie enough to give Big Dawg time to slam both weapons together against each of what was left of its ears. The zombie's head caved in, his milky eyes bulging out, hanging by the dried and decaying optic nerves.

Big Dawg jammed the pipe deep into the driver's chest, shoving his blackened heart out his back. It freed up Big Dawg's hand so he could grasp the eyeballs and yank them out. The creature howled through a mouth mostly collapsed from the head trauma, only to be shut up by Big Dawg slapping the eyeballs back down the zombie's throat, making sure to palm the deflating organs and not stick his fist in and risk slicing his hand open on the rotting teeth.

Big Dawg followed up with a backhand using the crescent wrench. He caught the monster beneath the chin, lifting the beast off its feet. The body landed with a sickening thud. The head sprang free and rang the bell, striking the halogen lamp high above with marksman precision before tumbling into the muddled pile of boxes.

Jessie and Gus were ready to go to town and beat some zombie ass. They had three of the undead coming at them. Then in the words of Pat Travers, "Boom! Boom! Out Go the Lights!"

"What the fuck?" Gus yelled as the zombie's head had crashed into the light and burst the lamp.

"Duck," Jessie commanded.

Gus didn't ask why. He just did as she said. As the trio of death clambered for the heads of the living, Jessie managed to turn on her light. Gus was beside her, squatted down. He brought the stock of the shotgun around, taking out the kneecap of another warehouse worker. It dropped the zombie to his own level that dragged a second zombie down with him, a woman in slacks and a blouse. Gus had his hands full alternating between the stock and the barrel, smacking the two. During his days of getting stoned, he and his buddies sat around and watched a lot of Bruce Lee and Chuck Norris movies. He wasn't a martial arts expert, but he seemed to be holding his own at the moment.

The third zombie had stepped past them. Jessie saw the scrawny figure dressed in a lab coat that had been white at one time. Now it looked more like it had been worn in a slaughterhouse as the creature stopped its ambling so it could turn and find its prey once more. She didn't know if it could actually see or not, but maybe it was just so stupid that when she ducked the zombie it took a moment for it to process the fact and react accordingly.

For quite some time now, Jessie had taken to carrying part of a microphone stand she had found backstage at the amphitheater years ago. She had removed the heavy base and just used the extendable pole, which was quite sturdy and had some heft to it. She had spent time, which she had plenty of, and repeatedly rubbed one end against stones and bricks, filing the tip down to a sharp cylinder. It was only the diameter of a quarter, but a razor-sharp quarter going into the body could do some major damage and leave a helluva a hole to plug.

The zombie took his first step back towards Jessie. She launched herself upwards from her crouched position, putting everything she had into her maneuver. She drove the sharpened stand underneath the chin, driving the makeshift spear through the toughened gray matter and smashing against the top of the cranium. Metal poked out through the top of the skull.

He tried to keep attacking but Jessie was a strong girl, much stronger than most would've guessed. She kept her balance with a back stance and her center of balance was low as she maintained her thrust on the pole. The opponents were at a standstill.

"You okay back there?" Gus asked between swings as he tried to stand upright and get an advantage over the two he battled.

"Yeah," she grunted. "Just doing a little trepanning."

"A little what?"

"Nevermind. How about you?" she asked, unable to turn around for fear of throwing herself off balance.

"Not" *thunk* "too" *whomp* "bad" *splat!* The man went down in a crumble of dust and bits, nothing left of his head. Gus's last swing had twisted him around. His foot slipped on a pile of dusty dead and flew out from beneath him. He went down, landing hard on his back and slamming his head on the concrete.

"Gus?" Jessie yelled. She was almost afraid to turn, positive she was going to see her cousin's head split wide open and coated in blood.

Gus didn't answer. He was out cold.

"Papa!" she yelled.

"I's a coming, baby girl," Alton Lee called back. His light was dying and he wasn't moving as fast as he wished he could.

Jessie gave a quick glance over her shoulder and saw Gus down and the secretary-type zombie hovering over him, preparing to bite into Gus's head. Jessie's adrenaline kicked in. She thrust forward then yanked back the pole with all her strength, ripping it free. The scientist moved her direction—and then fell down, face first into the floor without catching his fall. His face shattered against the concrete.

Jessie spun from her back stance to a front stance as she swung the pole, catching the secretary across the neck, bowling her over to the perimeter of the flashlight's glow. The creature let out a nasty hiss, shook its head and began to get up, hands outstretched and long, fake fingernails extended, clawing the air and her face was full of menace.

A chain wrapped around the woman's neck from behind. Alton Lee was trying to hold the hellcat in check while trying to keep her from scratching him, just in case those nails were contaminated because she was thrashing wildly trying to claw herself free. If his chain had been any shorter she would've been able to reach him. He kept it tightly about her neck and pulled down to keep her head back so she couldn't get enough leverage to turn and come at him.

"Damn, bitch! Chill yo ass out!" Alton Lee commanded, but she was heeding him no attention.

Jessie was bringing her pole back up to take a swing when a wrench flew from the darkness and nailed the side of the zombie's face, snapping her jaw and busting out several teeth. She relented for a moment, trying to scream, but it came out weak and garbled with her lower face missing. It was all the interference Alton Lee needed to snap her neck, twisting it until her head popped free.

"Now that's a lovely sound," Alton Lee said before kicking the head off into the darkness. "Gus okay or we's gonna have to kill his ass, too?"

Jessie returned to her cousin and looked him over. "I don't see any bites or claw marks. He hit the floor awfully hard. There's a little blood but not much." She shined her light in his eyes. The pupils contracted. "I think he'll be all right but it may take a while. He's definitely out."

Big Dawg strode up casual-like, an open box of Twinkies in one hand and one of the half-eaten snacks in the other as he munched it down.

"A bit stale, but tolerable," he said.

Alton Lee pulled some papers out of the lab coat of the dead scientist. He looked them over, bending down in front of Jessie's light, but they made no sense to him. He handed them to his daughter. She looked them over for a couple of minutes, her curiosity turning to shock and then anger.

"I'll be damned. This prick was one of a group of scientists secretly testing some new medicine, placing them in baked products and using the populous as their guinea pigs. These bastards started it."

"Then the Twinkies were a trap."

Big Dawg dropped his box and spit out what was in his mouth. He pulled out his flask and took a huge swig, swishing the burning liquid around in his mouth and spitting it out. He took another swig and downed it.

Their journey was for nothing, their battle unnecessary. Now they could do nothing but wait and see if Gus came to and if Big Dawg turned into Big Dead. While they did so, Jessie went prowling about in the offices with Big Dawg as her security. She found the secret lab the scientists had been using for nearly a year before the outbreak. They were paying someone under the table and weren't a part of the baking company in any sense of the word. Just some CEO who cared more for the big bucks than for people allowing experimental shit to happen. She secretly hoped he was ravaged and torn to tiny pieces one little bit at a time when the change happened.

She returned to the warehouse with Big Dawg, who was still a living, breathing, sentient being for the moment. Her father sat there near Gus, just staring at the avalanche of snacks. He was the first to hear the frightening noises.

The nerve-racking sound of several sets of fingernails etched into their brains through their eardrums from the high-pitched scraping down the metal bay doors. Unholy howls pierced the calmness of the night. Jessie suspected they were surrounded because the scarping was coming from every bay door. She wondered if they could escape and maybe make it to the Valero plant. If need be, they could make one final heroic attempt of exterminating the undead in a series of fiery explosions that would probably be seen for miles into Arkansas, Mississippi and across the expanse of Memphis. The Pyramid would think Ra had returned, only to discover Apep destroying the world and Anubis waiting at the gates with scale in hand.

ABOUT THE AUTHOR

Ethan Nahté spent several years working in TV & Film as well as some radio. His talents range from various positions in production and post-production to writing.

Ethan also worked as a professional journalist for several years, writing, editing and shooting photography primarily for entertainment magazines in North America and Europe, as well as newspapers and e-zines. He still does freelance work in all of the above vocations.

When not writing or taking spare moments to kick back and read, he spends most of his time hiking or fishing in the mountains and along the waterways of Arkansas and Oklahoma.

You can keep up with Ethan on his media site LiveNLoud.net, his official author site NahteWords.com, or at Facebook.com/ethannahtecreative

ABOUT THE COVER ARTIST

Artist **Mitchell Davidson Bentley** spent the last twenty years moving physically from place to place and artistically from traditional oils to cyber compositions. Trained in the traditional medium of oil by his mother, and inspired by his grandfather's love of science fiction, Bentley began his career as a full-time science fiction artist in 1989 from his home base in Tulsa.

While actively involved in the science fiction art world, Bentley also moved from Tulsa to Austin to Central Pennsylvania where his search for knowledge earned him bachelor's and master's degrees from Penn State University. Over the same period of time, Bentley shifted from the more traditional oil painting to airbrushed acrylics, and since 2004 has been working exclusively in electronic media.

As the Creative Consultant of Atomic Fly Studios, Bentley produces cover art, marketing materials and Web sites while he continues to produce quality 2D artwork marketed through the AFS Web site and at science fiction conventions across the United States.

Bentley has lectured at universities, worked in film (also as a part-time actor), edited publications and served as Artist Guest of Honor at more than a dozen science fiction conventions. He has also earned over 35 awards, and is a lifetime member of the Association of Science Fiction and Fantasy Artists.

He currently resides in Harrisburg, PA with his partner Cathie McCormick and their spoiled cats, Mr. Spike, Zöe and Drucilla.

Bentley's Web address is: www.atomicflystudios.com.

Yard Dog Press Titles As Of This Print Date

A Bubba in Time Saves None, Edited by Selina Rosen
A Man, A Plan, (yet lacking) A Canal, Panama, Linda Donahue
Adventures of the Irish Ninja, Selina Rosen
The Alamo and Zombies, Jean Stuntz
All the Marbles, Dusty Rainbolt
Almost Human, Gary Moreau
Ancient Enemy, Lee Killouth
The Anthology From Hell: Humorous Tales From WAY Down Under,
     Edited by Julia S. Mandala
Ard Magister, Laura J. Underwood
Assassins Inc., Phillip Drayer Duncan
Bad City, Selina Rosen & Laura J. Underwood
Bad Lands, Selina Rosen & Laura J. Underwood
Black Rage, Selina Rosen
Blackrose Avenue, Mark Shepherd
The Boat Man, Selina Rosen
Bobby's Troll, John Lance
Bride of Tranquility, Tracy S. Morris
Bruce and Roxanne from Start to Finnish, Rie Sheridan Rose
The Bubba Chronicles, Selina Rosen
Bubba Fables, Sue P. Sinor
Bubbas Of the Apocalypse, Edited by Selina Rosen
The Burden of the Crown, Selina Rosen
Chains of Redemption, Selina Rosen
Checking On Culture, Lee Killough
Chronicles of the Last War, Laura J. Underwood
Dadgum Martians Invade the Lucky Nickel Saloon, Ken Rand
Dark and Stormy Nights, Bradley H. Sinor
Deja Doo, Edited by Selina Rosen
Dracula's Lawyer, Julia S. Mandala
Dragon's Tongue, Laura J. Underwood
The Essence of Stone, Beverly A. Hale
Fairy BrewHaHa at the Lucky Nickel Saloon, Ken Rand
The Fantastikon: Tales of Wonder, Robin Wayne Bailey
Fire & Ice, Selina Rosen
Flush Fiction, Volume I: Stories To Be Read In One Sitting, Edited by
     Selina Rosen
Flush Fiction, Volume II: Twenty Years of Letting it Go!, Edited by
     Selina Rosen
The Four Bubbas of the Apocalypse: Flatulence, Halitosis, Incest,
     and... Ned, Edited by Selina Rosen
The Four Redheads: Apocalypse Now!, Linda L. Donahue, Rhonda
     Eudaly, Julia S. Mandala, & Dusty Rainbolt
The Four Redheads of the Apocalypse, Linda L. Donahue, Rhonda
     Eudaly, Julia S. Mandala, & Dusty Rainbolt

The Four Redheads: The Wrath of Satan, Linda L. Donahue,
   Rhonda Eudaly, Julia S. Mandala, & Dusty Rainbolt
The Garden In Bloom, Jeffrey Turner
The Geometries of Love: Poetry by Robin Wayne Bailey
The Golems Of Laramie County, Ken Rand
The Green Women, Laura J. Underwood
The Guardians, Lynn Abbey
Hammer Town, Selina Rosen
The Happiness Box, Beverly A. Hale
The Host Series: The Host, Fright Eater, Gang Approval, Selina
   Rosen
Houston, We've Got Bubbas!, Edited by Selina Rosen
How I Spent the Apocolypse, Selina Rosen
I Didn't Quite Make It To Oz, Edited by Selina Rosen
I Should Have Stayed In Oz, Edited by Selina Rosen
In the Shadows, Bradley H. Sinor
International House of Bubbas, Edited by Selina Rosen
It's the Great Bumpkin, Cletus Brown!, Katherine A. Turski
Judas Gene, Gary Moreau
The Killswitch Review, Steven-Elliot Altman & Diane DeKelb-
   Rittenhouse
The Leopard's Daughter, Lee Killough
The Lightning Horse, John Moore
The Logic of Departure, Mark W. Tiedemann
The Long, Cold Walk To Mars, Jeffrey Turner
Marking the Signs and Other Tales Of Mischief, Laura J. Underwood
Material Things, Selina Rosen
Medieval Misfits: Renaissance Rejects, Tracy S. Morris
Mirror Images, Susan Satterfield
Mirror, Mirror and Other Reflections, James K. Burk
More Stories That Won't Make Your Parents Hurl, Edited by Selina
   Rosen
Music for Four Hands, Louis Antonelli & Edward Morris
My Life with Geeks and Freaks, Claudia Christian
The Necronomicrap: A Guide To Your Horoooscope, Tim Frayser
Playing With Secrets, Bradley H & Sue P. Sinor
Redheads In Love, Linda L. Donahue, Rhonda Eudaly, Julia S.
   Mandala, & Dusty Rainbolt
Reruns, Selina Rosen
Rock 'n' Roll Universe, Ken Rand
Shadows In Green, Richard Dansky
Stories That Won't Make Your Parents Hurl, Edited by Selina Rosen
Tales from Keltora, Laura J. Underwood
*Tales Of the Lucky Nickel Saloon, Second Ave., Laramie, Wyoming, U
   S of A,* Ken Rand
Tarbox Station, Rhonda Eudaly

Texistani: Indo-Pak Food From A Texas Kitchen, Beverly A. Hale
That's All Folks, J. F. Gonzalez
Through Wyoming Eyes, Ken Rand
Turn Left to Tomorrow, Robin Wayne Bailey
The Twins, Selina Rosen
The Undead Ate My Head, Ethan Nahté
Wandering Lark, Laura J. Underwood
Weirdough, Inc., Selina Rosen & Sherri Dean
Wings of Morning, Katharine Eliska Kimbriel
Zombies In Oz and Other Undead Musings, Robin Wayne Bailey

Double Dog
(A YDP Imprint):

#1:
Of Stars & Shadows,
Mark W. Tiedemann
This Instance Of Me,
Jeffrey Turner

#2:
Gods and Other Children,
Bill D. Allen
Tranquility, Tracy Morris

#3:
Home Is the Hunter,
James K. Burk
Farstep Station,
Lazette Gifford

#4:
Sabre Dance,
Melanie Fletcher
The Lunari Mask,
Laura J. Underwood

#5:
House of Doors,
Julia Mandala
Jaguar Moon,
Linda A. Donahue

Just Cause
(A YDP Imprint):

The Bitter End
Selina Rosen

Death Under the Crescent Moon
Dusty Rainbolt

Getting It Real
Selina Rosen

The Ghost Writer
Selina Rosen

It's Not Rocket Science: Spirituality for the Working-Class Soul
Selina Rosen

Meditations of a Hoarder
Melinda LaFevers

Not My Life
Selina Rosen

The Pit
Selina Rosen

Plots and Protagonists: A Reference Guide for Writers
Mel. White

Vanishing Fame
Selina Rosen

Fantasy Writers Asylum
(A YDP Imprint):

Blood Songs
Julia Mandala
Gateway to Corimar
Julia Mandala & Linda L Donahue
Tale of the Black Heart
Linda L. Donahue

Non-YDP titles we distribute:

Chains of Freedom
Chains of Destruction
Jabone's Sword
Queen of Denial
Recycled
Strange Robby
Sword Masters
Selina Rosen

Three Ways to Order:

1. Write us a letter telling us what you want, then send it along with your check or money order (made payable to Yard Dog Press) to: Yard Dog Press, 710 W. Redbud Lane, Alma, AR 72921-7247

2. Use selinarosen@cox.net or lynnstran@cox.net to contact us and place your order. Then send your check or money order to the address above. *This has the advantage of allowing you to check on the availability of short-stock items such as T-shirts and back-issues of Yard Dog Comics.*

3. Contact us as in #1 or #2 above and pay with a credit card or by debit from your checking account. Either give us the credit card information in your letter/Email/phone call, or go to our website and use our shopping carts. If you send us your information, please include your name as it appears on the card, your credit card number, the expiration date, and the 3 or 4-digit security code after your signature on the back (CVV). Please remember that we will include media rate (minimum $3.00) S/H for mailing in the lower 48 states.

Watch our website at
www.yarddogpress.com
for news of upcoming projects
and new titles!!

A Note to Our Readers

We at Yard Dog Press understand that many people buy used books because they simply can't afford new ones. That said, and understanding that not everyone is made of money, we'd like you to know something that you may not have realized. Writers only make money on new books that sell. At the big houses a writer's entire future can hinge on the number of books they sell. While this isn't the case at Yard Dog Press, the honest truth is that when you sell or trade your book or let many people read it, the writer and the publishing house aren't making any money.

As much as we'd all like to believe that we can exist on love and sweet potato pie, the truth is we all need money to buy the things essential to our daily lives. Writers and publishers are no different.

We realize that these "freebies" and cheap books often turn people on to new writers and books that they wouldn't otherwise read. However we hope that you will reconsider selling your copy, and that if you trade it or let your friends borrow it, you also pass on the information that if they really like the author's work they should consider buying one of their books at full price sometime so that the writer can afford to continue to write work that entertains you.

We appreciate all our readers and *depend* upon their support.

Thanks,
The Editorial Staff
Yard Dog Press

PS – Please note that "used" books without covers have, in most cases, been stolen. Neither the author nor the publisher has made any money on these books because they were supposed to be pulped for lack of sales.

Please do not purchase books without covers.